THE DRAGON AND HER THIEF

ARIEL MARIE

Copyright © 2022 by Ariel Marie,
RNB Publishing, LLC

Cover by EmCat Designs

Edited by Dana Hook with Rebel, Edit & Design.

This is a work of fiction. Names, characters, organizations, businesses, events, and incidents are a figment of the author's imagination and are used fictitiously. Any similarities to real people, businesses, locations, history, and events are a coincidence.

Ebook ISBN: 978-1-956602-37-1

Paperback ISBN: 978-1-956602-28-9

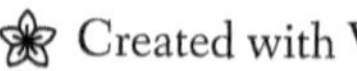 Created with Vellum

Preface

The Dragon and Her Thief was recently featured in the Cocky Alpha Shifters anthology. This story is now available for sale on its own. Please enjoy!

-Ariel Marie

The Dragon and Her Thief

A possessive dragon. A sexy thief. A job gone wrong...or did it?

Kelsey Rose wasn't crazy. She was determined. A family heirloom was stolen years ago, and she was the perfect person to recover it. No job was too big for her, but this one was going to be a challenge for her. The only obstacle?

A dragon shifter.

Mythia Zinfina spent centuries protecting and growing her hoard. The powerful dragon shifter was patiently waiting for the day she would find her mate. Never did she expect the tiny slip of a woman breaking into her castle to be the one who was destined to be at her side for all eternity.

The second their eyes met, Mythia's dragon determined she would never let Kelsey go.

If you love steamy, wlw paranormal romance tales with plenty of heat and action, then you will enjoy The Dragon and Her Thief. This story was intended for mature readers only.

CHAPTER ONE

"**Y**ou're crazy," Jasper growled. "This is a suicide mission."

Kelsey Rose raised her chin while resting her hands on her hips. She glanced around and saw the same incredulous look on everyone's faces.

Kelsey wasn't crazy.

Maybe a little stubborn and spontaneous, but she had all her marbles.

"It's the only time I'll be able to get in there and take back what rightfully belongs to my family."

Jasper and Kelsey's friendship dated back to when they were knee-high to a grasshopper. They had grown up on neighboring farms, and Jasper was the sibling she'd never had.

It was Friday, and as they always did to kick off their weekend, they met at the local hole-in-the-wall bar.

Frankie's was the place they could drink until they were barely able to walk.

They had a crowd surrounding them at the bar. The small town of Saxon Hills, Montana, had less than ten thousand residents, human and supernatural. All non-humans, from vampires to shifters' existence, had been revealed in the early twentieth century.

Their town's history dated back to the early nineteenth century, when Saxon Hills was settled. Kelsey's great great—she forgot how many greats—grandfather helped start the town. It was something she was proud of, but no one cared about history in these parts anymore.

"And if you're caught, you'll be as good as dead." Jasper slammed his empty mug on the counter. "Look, you may have dragon's blood in you—"

"That doesn't even count. I'm, like, one sixteenth on my mother's father's side,"

Kelsey declared. One of her mother's distant relatives mated with a dragon. Half of her children were shifters, the other human. But none of that mattered. What did matter was the mission she was planning.

Kevin, the town's drunk, spun around on his stool and faced them. "He's right."

Kelsey rolled her eyes. Of course he wanted to chime in on the conversation.

"Kevin, not now. Please." She held up a hand and shook her head as she took a seat on the stool next to Jasper.

"I may be a drunk, but I wasn't always this way." He let out a nasty belch. Kelsey grimaced and covered her nose with her hand. "She's an evil one, and won't hesitate to torture you and play with you like a toy. I've seen it with my own eyes." Kevin's gaze became unfocused, as if he was reliving some memory. Reaching out, he snagged his mug and brought the frosty beer to his lips.

He was referring to Mythia Zinfina, a powerful dragon shifter who had sworn to protect their town from evil. The billionaire had made her fortune over the centuries, getting rich off of her investments.

She resided in a castle in the mountains,

rarely coming down to mingle with the common folk.

And that's where she hid it, the Rose family medallion that was stolen from Kelsey's family, and she was determined to retrieve it.

She grinned. "But I won't get caught."

Jasper rolled his eyes and signaled for the barkeep. "Yeah, you say that now. This will be a little different from when we were younger." He leaned against the counter and focused his attention on her. A sigh escaped him, as he must have realized she was serious. "Okay. Even if you were able to get inside that monstrous castle, how are you going to get inside her vault? This is a dragon shifter you're talking about. A very powerful one at that."

She elbowed him playfully. "You let me worry about that." A plan was slowly forming in her mind. "I just need a distraction, and I know you're good for it."

"Me?" he chirped, his eyebrows jerking up. The barkeep arrived, and he ordered them another round before turning his attention back to her. "Look, Kelsey, I love you like a sister, but I don't know if I can risk it."

"Really? What are you risking?" She blew out an exasperated breath. When did her friend turn soft? When they were teenagers, they were constantly in trouble with the sheriff, who was on a first-name basis with their parents.

"Well, for one, I'm too pretty to go to jail."

Everyone in the group laughed, but she snorted. Her friend was sort of a manwhore. "Who told you that?"

Not that she could talk.

They used to bet on who could pull the most girls on nights the bar scene was dull.

She had more notches on her bedpost than him. Some chicks jumped at the chance of a one-night stand with her. They were always curious as to what it would be like having sex with a woman.

She didn't mind, because most times, all she was looking for was a good time with no strings attached.

"Your mother mentioned it once."

She shoved his shoulder. "You were sixteen and had a baby face. Now you're thirty-five with—"

"A great job, a big dick, and never a cold bed."

"Oh, God. I do not want to hear about your dick." The barkeep returned and dropped their frothy beers in front of them. She grabbed hers and took a healthy sip. "Besides, I'm sure I have a strap-on bigger than you."

Jasper choked on his beer as they all fell into a fit of laughter. Jasper wiped his face, tears streaming down his cheeks.

"And I don't want to hear about your strap-ons."

She loved her best friend. She didn't know what she would do without him.

"Well, if Jasper here is too chicken to cause a distraction, I'm sure me and the fellas could do it for you," Kevin offered.

Kelsey spun around and stared at the small group of men that surrounded her. These were men who worked at the factory with her and Jasper.

"I'm not asking for anything dangerous. It could be made to look like kids play," she said, taking a sip of her beer. "Don, you sure Kathy won't box your ears?"

"My wife will be fine. You let me worry about her."

She forced herself not to snort. Everyone knew Kathy wore the pants in the family.

Instead, she cocked her brow and asked, "Don, you sure?"

"Hell yeah," he replied, folding his arms across his burly chest. "I would love to see that dragon get knocked off her pedestal."

"I have a few fireworks and explosives left over from last July," Harvey offered.

"We're in, Kelsey. Let's get your family heirloom back," Alfie said.

All eyes turned to Jasper, who was the only one who hadn't committed. He paused, his mug an inch from his lips. With her best pleading, puppy dog eyes, she watched him slowly set down his beer.

"Fine. I'm in," he groaned, throwing his hands up in defeat. Kelsey jumped from her chair and threw her arms around his neck, squeezing him in a tight hug.

"Thank you." She pressed a hard kiss to his cheek before letting him go. "You guys are the best."

"There's a meeting of the mighty dragons on Sunday night," James volunteered.

"We'll wait until she leaves," Kelsey started. They would need a strong plan. Once the oversized onyx dragon flew across the sky, they would wait. The distraction would be for the castle employees.

If they were going to steal from a dragon, the best time would be when the dragon wasn't there.

Kelsey would be in and out before anyone would know any better.

Wrapping a towel around her body, Kelsey exited her bathroom and stepped into her bedroom. She was bone tired, and still tipsy from drinking with Jasper.

She moved over to the window, pushed the curtains aside, and stared up into the dark night. There wasn't a cloud in sight. The midnight sky was open, with little twinkling stars. It looked magical.

Off in the distance was the castle. Her target.

Kelsey was raised by her single mother and grandmother, never having met her father. He had disappeared when her mother was pregnant with her. From the time she was a young child, her mother had spoken of the ruby medallion that was stolen by the Zinfina family.

"It was a beautiful rose made of ruby, with a real silver chain," her mother had shared.

Kelsey had to be about eight years old when she began speaking of her family tree. Their family had once been prosperous members of the community and loved by everyone in Saxon Hills. Her great grandfather was once mayor of the town.

Over the years, their family had been hit with hard times. Her mother, Delaney, still owned the Rose Farm, a cattle ranch. Her mother and grandmother ran it and were doing well.

Suddenly, a shadow of a magnificent dragon appeared in the sky, making her gasp. She leaned forward and pressed her nose to the window.

"What did it feel like to fly?" she whispered aloud.

Closing her eyes, she imagined riding on the back of the dragon with the wind in her hair and the world at her feet.

She would be foolish to try and deny she hadn't moved into her small apartment because of the location to the castle.

She blinked and returned her attention back to the sky, but the dragon was no longer there.

Mythia.

Kelsey had never spoken with the shifter, and had only seen her from afar. She was tall and curvaceous, with brown skin and dark hair that flowed past her shoulders.

The Zinfina family was rich beyond Kelsey's wildest dreams.

"They better be," Kelsey muttered. That would just be dumb if they hadn't collected wealth through the centuries.

She turned away from the window and walked over to her closet, removed the towel, and hung it up on its hook. The cool air of her central air caused goosebumps to form on her skin and her nipples to pebble. She snagged the nightshirt off her bed and threw it on.

Her eyes landed on the black duffle bag that sat on the floor of her closet. Grabbing it, she set it on her bed and unzipped it to peer inside.

All the tools she would need to break open a vault were there. She had been collecting them for months. After her extensive research on vaults, she was confident she would be able to break into it.

No one knew what type of vault the dragon would have.

Considering the age of the castle, Kelsey was banking on the vault being old as well, which would make it easy for her to crack.

The dragon shifter's castle had stood for centuries.

"She won't even know what hit her," Kelsey murmured, grinning as she zipped the bag shut.

Soon, the Rose medallion would be home. She couldn't wait to turn it over to her mother, who had a collection of family items handed down to her from previous generations. It was like a family museum in their basement.

She smiled.

Her mother was going to be shocked when she placed that ruby medallion in her hand.

CHAPTER TWO

"And you're certain of this?" Mythia Zinfina snapped, staring at the seer with a hard gaze. She had been summoned back to the castle from her evening flight, and her beast wasn't pleased they'd had to cut their flight short.

It felt good to stretch her wings and glide through the midnight air. She would have been out for hours, but she received a message to return to the castle immediately.

Apparently, there was something Sascha had seen in a vision. What she had shared with Mythia was that she had seen Mythia's mate.

Mythia had scoured this world over a thousand times, and had yet to find the one the fates designed for her.

After all the long years she had searched, she was ready to give up, content to fly through the skies alone for the rest of her life.

Her dragon huffed at her dramatic nature.

Shut it, she warned. Her animal knew her true nature. Saying she was giving up on finding her mate was a fib.

A dragon never stopped searching and preparing for their mate.

"Yes, my lady." Sascha bowed her head, her long silver hair falling forward. Her skin, a russet reddish-brown, was smooth for a woman nearing a hundred. Sascha was blessed with good genes, with almost no wrinkles on her face. It had to be the powers of her people that kept her looking so young. She was still young compared to Mythia.

Sascha began working for Mythia ages ago, when she was a young girl of twenty. She had come to trust the seer, who rarely had visions that didn't come true.

Mythia moved to stand in front of the roaring fire. Even in the fall, the mountains in

Montana were slightly chilly. The castle was centuries old, and she'd had it renovated to bring it to the modern age. It was decked out with the best technology money could buy.

But one thing that never ceased to amaze her was the slight chill that always lingered in the air.

She stared into the flames, excitement filling her chest.

Her dragon was ready to prepare their home.

She thought of all the treasures she had stored away to present to her mate, and could only pray it would be enough.

"Tell me again, what did you see?" she demanded. She needed to know everything she could about her mate before her arrival. Mythia turned and motioned to the high-back chair positioned in front of the stone hearth.

Sascha appeared to float past her. Mythia sat in the chair next to her and crossed her leather encased legs in preparation for the story.

"She's a beautiful young woman," Sacha began, offering Mythia a small smile. "She has warm bronze skin, long brown hair, and big brown eyes. She loves the outdoors. I saw her farming and working in a factory."

Mythia nodded. Of course her mate would be a hard worker, and a lover of the outdoors was right up Mythia's alley. Sacha's description of her mate was generic, but it didn't matter.

Any woman sent by the fates was bound to be beautiful.

"How do we meet?" she asked.

"It will be here, at the castle."

How was that even possible? There were no events planned at her home.

"What business will she have here at the castle?" Mythia frowned. She hosted an event once a year where she could mingle with the townsfolk she had pledged hundreds of years ago to protect. Over the years, multiple dragons have tried to overtake Saxon Hills.

It was a pledge she would fight tooth and nail for.

She'd always had a soft spot for it. One of the founders of the town, Paxton Rose, had made her swear that she would always keep this town under her wing. According to him, she was the only one he would trust with the future of his people and his family. He was a great friend, and she had mourned his death.

"Oh, it will be soon, Mythia. In two days' time, your mate will sneak into the castle. She's on a mission."

That caught Mythia's attention. Her dragon prowled around inside of her chest.

Why would anyone sneak into the castle? Unless... they were going to steal something?

She snarled.

A thief.

Her mate was a thief?

She stood abruptly from her chair, almost knocking it over.

"You mean to tell me that my mate is coming to steal from me?" She swung around and faced Sascha, her heart pounding at the thought of someone trying to steal everything she had collected over the years.

What honor was there in stealing?

"There is something she seeks that she believes belongs to her family." Sascha stood up with a grin spreading across her face, her long skirt billowing around her feet. "I have set a little trap for your mate. She thinks you will be gone away for business."

Mythia rested her hands on her waist. "I'm not scheduled for anything."

"I know," Sascha giggled. "But the humans think you are going off to some elaborate meeting of dragons."

"Why would the fates see fit to give me a thief?" Mythia began to pace in front of the fireplace. What had she done in life to warrant being matched with someone dishonorable? "There's nothing in my castle that belongs to anyone else."

"From what I can see in my visions, she's not a bad person."

Mythia whirled around and stared at her seer. "How many have you had?"

"A few. I wanted to make sure I was absolutely sure of who she was." Sascha met her glare head on, and Mythia relaxed slightly. "I would never deceive you, my lady."

"I know that." Mythia sighed. "What are we to do?"

"Like I said, she is going to break into the castle soon. You will need to be ready for her."

Mythia nodded. She would be ready for her little mate.

A thief?

Mythia would have to teach her woman a lesson. She was rich, having lived for centuries. There would be no need for the woman to steal ever again.

Mythia would lay the world at her feet.

"Can you show me what you saw?" Mythia whispered.

"I can try." Sascha stepped in front of her and pressed her fingertips to Mythia's forehead. Warmth spread across Mythia's skin, and she gasped once she closed her eyes.

An image of the most beautiful woman appeared.

Big brown eyes. Long, luscious dark hair. Ruby red lips.

It was an image of her on what looked to be a farm. She smiled and looked up at the sky.

Then the vision disappeared.

Mythia's heart rate began to increase. She memorized every feature of her mate, barely able to contain her excitement at finally meeting her in person.

Her dragon was an impatient beast. Two days was a long time to wait. She had searched for years for her, and now she learned the woman had been right up under her nose the whole time.

She opened her eyes and found Sascha staring at her.

"Don't go searching for her."

Either she had seen a vision, or she just knew Mythia well.

"Did you see—"

"No vision. I just know you, Mythia Zinfina." Grinning, she patted Mythia's arm. "Be patient. You've waited a thousand years to find her. Let her come to you."

* * *

Mythia walked along the many priceless items she had collected over the years. Gold, diamonds, and paintings were just some of the treasures that filled the massive room. She reached down and plucked a gold Spanish coin from the sixteenth century. There was an oversized basket filled with them. The shield on the coin was that of Philip the Prudent, who had offered her payment with baskets of gold coins for her services.

Back in those times, those coming into

power had dragons on their side. It was with her help he was able to claim some of his territories.

She remembered it as if it were yesterday.

Time sure flies by when you're having fun.

Mythia didn't regret any timeline in her past. She was blessed to be a dragon shifter who had lived a long life.

Her mate, once she consumed Mythia's blood, would be able to live a long life at her side. Her blood would stop her mate's aging process, and she'd always appear to be the age she currently was.

Mythia tossed the coin back and continued. The room was a few stories tall and hidden deep in the mountains. Her dragon begged to be released so she could fly around town to try to catch a glimpse of their mate.

"No. You heard what Sascha said. Let her come to us." She stopped in front of one of the oil paintings she'd purchased in the seventeenth century.

Mate. We need her.

"I know, but Sascha was right. We can wait two days." She took in the canvas that depicted two naked women lying on a plush chaise. A slim one with curly hair and high breasts sat wrapped up in the arms of a curvaceous redhead. It was an intimate painting that depicted the beauty of two women together.

She smiled at all the emotions that swirled around in her chest. This painting had been hard to find, for lesbian sexuality was not accepted then. Many laws had been proposed by politicians here in the U.S., but Mythia couldn't remember if any had ever become a law.

She snorted. They were all hypocrites.

Those politicians only wanted to pretend to work for the greater good when she knew quite a few of them participated in couplings with other men behind closed doors.

She'd had to hunt the artist down and paid her a handsome amount for the picture.

Mythia took one last look at the treasure she had collected for almost a millennium. She spun on her heel and walked out of the room, hit the keypad on the wall by the door, and watched it slowly close.

She prided herself on the updated technology. Her priceless treasure had to be protected.

The door slammed shut, the sound echoing down the hall.

She stalked down the hallway to prepare for the arrival of her mate. Anticipation made her walk faster.

Her little thief thought she would sneak in and steal from her?

Mythia would gladly teach her a lesson she would never forget.

CHAPTER THREE

Kelsey stared up at the magnificent dragon gliding through the sky. The massive wingspan was mesmerizing. From her position on the ground, the animal appeared smaller, but Kelsey knew the beast was larger than any land animal.

Butterflies appeared in her stomach. She didn't know why, but she felt drawn to the dragon. She had always had a fascination with such mystical creatures. She *was* raised in a community of shifters and humans.

But dragons? Secretly, they had always

been her favorite. She didn't know one personally, but she'd always admired them from afar.

It was something about their power.

Their magic.

Their strength.

"That's our cue," Jasper announced, breaking through Kelsey's thoughts. He hit the hood of his truck and jogged over to the driver's door.

Kelsey tore her eyes away from the dragon as she got smaller the farther away she flew.

They had one night.

According to the information she'd heard, Mythia would return by morning.

Kelsey walked over and got into the passenger seat, slammed the door, and buckled her seat belt.

"Are you sure about this?" Jasper asked. In the low light, she could see his raised eyebrows. Her friend had been trying to talk her out of this since she first mentioned her plan.

"Yes, I'm sure." Getting her family heirloom back was important. She rubbed her hands on her black leggings. She knew this was different from the juvenile break-in pranks from their youth. The only times she had ever gotten caught were when someone ratted her out. She had been quite good at it, and was sure she could pull it off. "For the thousandth time, this means a lot to me."

"Have you ever wondered why no one in your family before you tried to get it back?" he asked, starting the engine. The two of them were to meet the rest of the group at the base of the mountain.

"Because no one has big balls like me?" she snickered.

"You got that right." He shook his head and pulled away from the parking spot. They drove through town in silence, with Kelsey settled back in her seat. It had been easy to get her hands on the plans of the castle. They were public record.

She would enter through an entrance in the back of the castle, which would require her to traipse through the woods near the cliff. She had been through there before when she was younger.

All the kids participated in daring each other to get as close to the castle as possible, and that's why they went with using kids as a distraction.

The fellas would set off fireworks and gain the attention of security, allowing her to slip into the structure unseen.

It would work.

"There they are." Jasper jerked his chin toward two extended cab pickup trucks parked along the edge of the road. Kelsey hit the button to her window and rolled it down once Jasper pulled up alongside the first one.

Harvey grinned at her. "Howdy."

"Hey," she replied. Harvey's face was painted in green and brown, as if he was going off to war. From what she could see, they were all dressed in dark clothes and fatigues. "Y'all ready to go?"

"We sure are, boss," Kevin called out from inside the truck. She prayed he was sober since they were dealing with explosives. Fireworks and alcohol did not go together.

"You haven't been drinking, have you?" she asked.

"I'm as sober as a nun." He laughed. "Now, after a successful gig, drinks are on me."

"Hear, hear!" the guys cheered. Kelsey didn't care what they got up to after they did their job. She could take it the rest of the way.

"Now remember, if you're caught—"

"We don't know nothin' and was just havin' fun," Don said from the passenger seat. He sat forward to get a look at her and whistled. "Look at you. Our little cat burglar."

She rolled her eyes. She wore a black tunic, leggings, sturdy boots—since she would be going through the woods—and her hair pulled up in a high bun.

Glancing at her outfit, she sighed.

Maybe he was right.

"The rendezvous point for you will be where you drop me off." She turned to Jasper. "Give me an hour. I promise, if I don't find it, I'll leave."

"One hour from the time I drop you off?"

She bit her lip. She might need a little more time. She looked down at her phone to see it was a little after ten.

"If I'm not back by midnight, leave."

"What? No way." Jasper shook his head

furiously. "Hell no. If you don't come out, I'm going in to get you."

"No!" she barked, holding up her hand. "I don't want anyone to get into trouble. I'll be fine. What's the worst someone could do? Call the cops on me?" She wasn't afraid of going to jail. It'd been a while since she'd had a good ol' conversation with the sheriff. As she'd gotten older, she'd changed her life and hadn't been arrested since she was twenty-one, and that had been for public intoxication. They had hit the bars for her birthday, and things had gotten out of hand.

She was thirty-five now, so hopefully Sheriff Brack would go easy on her. She had become a model citizen who held down a good job at the local factory and helped her family on the farm.

Tightening his jaw, Jasper ran a hand through his thick hair.

"I don't like this," he said.

"I'll be fine. We're moving forward with the plan." She rested a hand on the back of his. She softened slightly, because he was always looking out for her. He was the closest thing to a brother she had. "I can take care of myself."

"Whenever you say that, the shit always hits the fan."

She barked out a laugh and waved him off.

"All right, men. Let's move out!"

* * *

Kelsey leaned against a tree while she waited. She had canvased the area and didn't see any signs of security.

"This is just too easy," she murmured. One would think security would be patrolling the area or something. But then again, who would be crazy enough to break into a dragon's lair and steal from them?

She chuckled.

Nope, she still wasn't crazy. Just determined.

Maybe the security system was invisible. Or maybe they used magic. If there was a ward around the property, she was sure they would have come running once she got close to the building.

She glanced around and still, nothing.

Kelsey hefted her backpack on her shoulders, prepared to wait for the signal. If she could pull this off, her mother and grand-mother will be so happy to have their family heirloom back. This would also be the greatest little heist she'd ever accomplished.

Her childhood burglaries were nothing of this magnitude, but the young girl inside her was cheering her on. She was competitive by nature.

She thought of what Jasper's face would look like when she strolled up to his truck at the rendezvous point with her prize in hand.

Kelsey checked her phone and saw there was a minute until they were to start. She slid it back into her bag and knelt, ready to haul ass across the yard.

"Come on, guys. Don't let me down." She kept her eyes on the entrance, praying no one would come out of it. The distraction was in the front, so the hope was that security would go out the other doors.

Her muscles tensed.

Boom!

She hesitated for ten seconds. Shouting could be heard off in the distance, and she grinned.

Perfect.

She took off across the grass, her arms

pumping, until her feet hit the concrete walkway. She skidded to a halt and knelt by the door. She reached behind her and pulled out her lock picking set while she eyed the lock.

Kelsey positioned herself in front of the door and reached for the handle.

"I'll be damned," she breathed.

The door was unlocked.

What in the hell?

She looked around to see if she had been caught unaware.

Boom!

Time for her to go.

Putting her kit away, she swung open the door and walked inside, closing it quietly behind her. When she had received the blueprints for the castle, she had memorized the route to the vault. She was sure over time, some things had changed, but it was amazing that the plans were so easily available in the zoning office. She had given an excuse of just researching the founding of the town, and the clerk had handed her a copy.

She took a look around and recognized the servant areas. She walked down the hallway and paused.

Left.

She strolled down the winding halls, careful not to make any noise. When she came upon a large set of wooden doors, she stared at them with a grin on her lips.

This was it. Just as the plans had revealed. This would lead her down to the lower level where the vault was said to be kept.

Her heart rate spiked.

She opened one door and slipped inside. There was a wide, winding staircase with lit scones on the stone walls.

"Wow." She immediately felt as if she were being transported back in time as she began her descent to the lower level. There was a slight chill in the air that made the hairs on the back of her neck stand up.

Arriving at the lower level, she found herself in a foyer of sorts, with a slate tiled floor that was more modern than she expected. She crept forward and took in the room off to the side. There was a small fireplace that was empty and dark. A thick cream shag rug was placed in front of the hearth. The room looked as if it were a small library. Shelves filled with old books lined the walls. The medieval architecture showed off the spectacular woodwork. She breathed in the smell of books and sighed, and her eyes landed on a large chaise built into the wall.

Backing away, she turned, and her target came into view.

The vault.

"Wait a minute." She strode over to it, fear mounting in her chest. This wasn't an old vault hundreds of years old. "Dammit."

The door was enforced steel, with an elaborate electronic keypad that was far beyond her means of getting into as a petty thief. The panel on the wall next to the door looked like something out of the movies. The little tools in her bag wouldn't even put a small dent in the steel.

What did you really think? The dragon would remain back in the olden days?

Kelsey's shoulders slumped. It didn't look as if she was breaking into a vault and retrieving anything tonight. She was going to have to come up with another plan.

"Fuck." She didn't like the feeling of defeat. She gripped the handles of her bag and went back into the library. Her eyes swept the area again before she continued into the room.

The shelves of books were interesting. Some appeared to be hundreds of years old. Seeing how the dragon shifter was just as old, it made sense.

Kelsey continued strolling along. This room was fascinating. There were some artifacts that should've been in museums. Kelsey was no expert, but the items looked as if they would be worth a shit ton of money.

One item in particular caught her attention. Sitting on a stand, covered in a black velvet material, was a medallion made of red ruby.

"It can't be," she whispered. Her pulse pounded at the sight of the beautiful piece of jewelry. It was just as her mother had described. "Unbelievable."

This was truly too easy.

It had to mean she was meant to reclaim this for her family.

She reached for it.

"I wouldn't do that if I were you," a husky voice called out from behind her.

Kelsey paused, the sound of the woman's voice washing over her. A tingling sensation rippled through her body. The sound of her roaring blood filled her ears. Kelsey jerked her arm back.

What the hell was she going to do?

"Put your hands up where I can see them," the woman commanded.

This must be security. She should've just left the moment she saw the vault was too complicated, but her curiosity got the better of her.

"I haven't taken anything," Kelsey said. Hopefully, this would make things go easier. She could possibly talk the woman into letting her go. She raised her empty hands in the air.

"Turn around. Slowly."

Swallowing hard, Kelsey did as she was ordered. Her gaze landed on the owner of the voice and her eyes widened.

Mythia.

If she was standing here, then who was the dragon who flew off earlier? Mythia's amber eyes glowed, the light from the scones shining off her warm brown skin. Her body was covered in leather, as if she were poured into it. Her feet were encased in heels, and her long dark hair flowed around her shoulders.

She narrowed her eyes on Kelsey.

Instantly, Kelsey knew she was in trouble.

Her breaths were starting to come fast, and her core pulsed. There was something about this woman. She was unsure as to why she was reacting the way she was.

Mythia took her time as she ambled into the room toward her.

Did the dragon shifter place her under a spell?

Kelsey blinked. No. There was no spell or witchcraft involved. The dragon shifter was just hot as hell.

Her hips swayed like a confident goddess.

Kelsey was unable to take her eyes off the woman. This was the closest she had ever been to the shifter, and her mouth went dry.

Kelsey's gaze moved down to her ample breasts straining against the leather tunic, the swell of them exposed by the low-cut neckline.

Stopping in front of her, Mythia tipped her chin up with a single finger.

The heat blazing in those amber eyes confirmed it.

She was in trouble.

Only, she had a feeling she was going to like it.

CHAPTER FOUR

"What is your name?" Mythia asked, inhaling the scent of her mate. She had to fight down her dragon as she roared, its magic swirling around inside of her.

"Kelsey." Her lip trembled slightly. Mythia watched, fascinated, as her pupils dilated. The scent of her arousal was faint, but growing. She inhaled sharply, fighting to keep her fangs from descending.

Yes, her mate was reacting to her.

She wasn't sure how, since Kelsey was human. She had never heard of a human recognizing their mate.

Or maybe it was her attraction to Mythia revealing itself.

"And what should I do with you, little thief?" She slid her thumb along Kelsey's bottom lip. Up close, she could see her mate's true beauty. The woman was a knockout. She had never seen her before, and was surprised, since the town of Saxon Hills was small.

But then again, she didn't fraternize with the locals often, so how would she have met this young woman?

"Um, let me go?" The hope in Kelsey's voice was laughable.

Oh, no.

She would never let her go.

"That's not possible. You've broken into my home and were about to take something that doesn't belong to you."

"Well, see, that's the thing. I entered an open door and was looking—"

Mythia placed a single finger on Kelsey's plump, kissable lips.

Mate.

Claim her.

Dragons were possessive creatures by nature, and would do anything to protect their mate.

Even kill.

"It doesn't matter how you spin it. You entered my home uninvited, dressed in all black like a..." She trailed off, trying to think of the modern-day term. "A cat burglar."

"Everyone's got jokes," Kelsey muttered.

"Drop the bag," she ordered. She'd had two days to plan her meeting with her mate, and the punishment that would come along with breaking and entering into the castle.

"Look, if you want to call the police, I won't try to run. I'll admit I came in unannounced, but I didn't take anything." Kelsey removed the bag and dropped it onto the floor in front of her. "You can search my bag if you'd like."

"That won't be necessary." Mythia moved the bag out of the way with her foot. "Place your hands behind your back."

"Sheriff Brack will see to it that I'm punished. It's been a while since I've been arrested—"

"This isn't your first time breaking into someone's house?"

"When I was a kid. Nothing in a long while, though. You know how kids are, pulling pranks and daring others to do something."

"But you're a grown woman now."

Lifting her hand, Mythia gave a slight flick of her wrist. Using her dragon's magic, she restrained her mate's hands in place.

"What the—" Kelsey began struggling against the magical hold around her wrists.

"Don't struggle too hard, or it will tighten." Slowly walking around her mate, she took in her wide hips. Her thighs were muscular and toned. Her waist was narrow, and her large breasts were evident beneath her dark shirt.

Mythia reached out and undid the bun Kelsey had her hair in, watching in wonder as it spread out along her shoulders. It was thick, gorgeous hair, with light blonde streaks running through her dark tresses.

Kelsey stood still, her eyes taking in Mythia as she walked around her. Mythia was extremely pleased at what she saw. Maybe fate had it right. She could certainly overlook the thievery if it wasn't a common occurrence.

Mythia couldn't care less.

All that mattered was that her mate was here with her.

"What are you going to do with me?" Her breathless question lit a fire inside of Mythia. Her dragon roared inside of her, pressing for Mythia to let her out.

Claim her.

Mythia's fingertips grew warm from her magic.

"I'm glad you asked." Her lips spread into a wide grin. Turning from Kelsey, she blew a gust of air toward the fireplace.

Instantly, a roaring fire appeared. She glanced at the door that snapped shut and locked.

Now she had her mate all to herself.

Kelsey's audible gulp met her ears.

She rested two fingers on Kelsey's sternum.

"Punish you."

Kelsey glanced down and gasped. Her clothes and boots were no longer on her body. She stood before Mythia, naked.

Mythia greedily took in Kelsey's perfect body. Her high breasts with her rosy areolas, her nipples puckered into hard beads.

"How?" Kelsey looked up, amazed.

"How? Is that what you ask, not why?" Mythia reached for her breasts and cupped them with her hands. She rubbed the soft skin and bit back a growl. They were perfectly shaped and overfilled her hands.

"I meant to ask that too," she breathed.

Mythia tugged on her nipple, eliciting another gasp. Her mate's arousal was growing, and the scent was driving Mythia insane.

Mythia leaned down and nuzzled her face in the crook of Kelsey's neck, celebrating the fact that her mate wasn't attempting to resist or fight her. She trailed her tongue along the column of Kelsey's neck.

Her animal rumbled in her chest as she continued to tug and tease Kelsey's nipples.

"How? Because I'm a fucking dragon shifter who used the magic the gods have charged me with." She nipped Kelsey's neck. Her mate's body trembled beneath her hands, and she loved it. She dropped her hands down to Kelsey's waist, taking in her soft, smooth skin.

Continuing down, Mythia moved her hands to Kelsey's ass and squeezed as she pressed Kelsey closer to her. Taking advantage of their closeness, she trailed her tongue up her neck and along her jawline, taking little nips as she moved to Kelsey's lips.

Kelsey whimpered, and the sound went straight to Mythia's core. Her pussy was dripping wet. She couldn't wait to feel her mate's tongue slide inside of her slit and lap up all her juices.

"Why? Because you deserve this for trying to steal from me."

She took Kelsey's lips in a hard, brutal kiss. She slid her a hand to the back of Kelsey's neck to hold her still while she plundered her mouth. Her tongue swept inside of Kelsey's parted lips, demanding entrance.

Mythia had never had to beg for anything in her life.

What she wanted, she took.

Tonight would be the same.

She wanted her mate, and she was going to have her.

Kelsey returned the kiss with the same heated passion that burned in Mythia's chest. It had to be the work of fate. There was never a time she had heard of in her long life that a human felt the mating call. They always fell in love with their soul mates.

What made her mate so special?

She would definitely question Sascha about it later.

Much later.

Mythia released Kelsey's mouth. They stared at each other, both of them breathing hard.

"Free my hands." Kelsey's brown eyes were so dark, they were almost black.

"Not a chance. I'm in charge." Mythia nipped Kelsey's bottom lip. Threading her fingers through Kelsey's thick locks to hold her in place, she placed her other hand on Kelsey's mons. "Do you understand?"

Mythia pushed her finger into her slit and was met with a drenched pussy. She gave a slight rub to Kelsey's clit.

Kelsey's eyes fluttered closed as she whimpered.

Mythia tightened her grip and bent her head back farther. The new position, with her hands behind her back, lifted her breasts higher in the air. Mythia growled.

This beautiful creature was hers.

She leaned down and trailed her tongue along the full length of her neck.

"Answer me." She nipped Kelsey on the

shoulder, but not enough to leave a mark. Soon, she would claim her mate.

In this exact spot.

But for now, she had to show her mate the error of her ways.

She flicked Kelsey's clit again, eliciting another gasp.

"Oh, God." Kelsey's breasts were rising and falling with each breath she took.

"I'm waiting, Kelsey," Mythia growled.

"Yes... I understand," she responded breathlessly.

"Good. I'm going to ensure you receive the punishment you deserve and need." Mythia pushed her fingers farther along Kelsey's slit. Her legs parted slightly to allow Mythia to explore her. "Since you broke into my home, you will not be allowed to climax. I own your pleasure."

A long, drawn-out moan escaped Kelsey's lips. Mythia paused her fingers and brought them up to her lips, relaxing her hold on Kelsey's hair.

Her mate's brown eyes flew open and watched as Mythia licked her lips clean. The exquisite taste of her mate burst forth on her tongue. She needed more.

Mythia pressed closer to her, brushing her lips along Kelsey's.

"You belong to me now."

Unable to resist, she claimed Kelsey's mouth again, holding tight to her hair. Her core pulsed when Kelsey's tongue began dancing with hers.

With her free hand, Mythia pinched and tugged hard on her nipple.

Kelsey tore her mouth away from Mythia's and cried out.

"Come." Mythia walked her captive mate over to the rug in front of the blazing fire and pushed her down onto her knees.

Kelsey looked up at her. The image of her mate restrained, kneeling naked before her, would forever be etched into her memories for as long as she lived.

This would not be the last time. She would take great care of her mate to ensure she had everything she deserved.

Mythia snapped her fingers, and her clothes vanished from her body.

The warmth of the flames caressed her naked skin as her mate's eyes roamed up and down her body.

Resting her hands on her hips, Mythia

planted her feet apart, wanting her mate to see all of her. The flare of desire in her eyes displayed she was pleased with what she saw.

Mythia would always want to ensure her mate was pleased. That would be her life's mission. Everything would be for Kelsey.

She took her mate by the hair and brought her face to her pussy.

"Go ahead. Taste my cunt," Mythia ordered. Her protruding clit was already swollen and sensitive. Kelsey leaned forward and licked at her clit, causing Mythia to groan in pleasure as she held Kelsey's hair in a firm grip. "Suck it."

Kelsey closed her lips around it and sucked. Mythia's body shook when the woman took firm hold of it and tugged on her sensitive bud.

Mythia cried out. Her hips pressed forward while she held Kelsey in place. Her mate's tongue was wicked. She didn't need much guidance.

"Enough." Mythia had to get a hold of herself. This was moving entirely too fast. She had her mate, and they had their entire lives together. She refused to climax so quickly the first time she got to fuck her.

She gave a gentle push to Kelsey's shoulder.

Kelsey yelped and fell backward onto the rug, her hands still cuffed behind her. She laid spread eagle on the floor. The sight of her pink pussy, with a slight sheen of moisture, almost had Mythia falling to her knees.

She needs to be punished first. Understand what she did wrong.

"Roll over to your stomach," Mythia commanded. Kelsey gave a nod and did as she was told. It pleased Mythia greatly how quick her mate understood obedience. Mythia knelt beside her. "Lift up onto your knees."

With a blink, Mythia released the hold on Kelsey's wrists. Her mate immediately brought her arms around and positioned her ass in the air while resting her head on the rug.

The flicking light from the fire and candles gave her a perfect view of her mate's core.

Her ass was beautiful and round. Mythia's hand skated along the soft flesh, her eyes zeroing in on Kelsey's puckered rim. Leaning forward, she gripped both cheeks and massaged them. She then ran her tongue along Kelsey's plump cheeks before making her way to her dark hole, bathing the little rim with her tongue.

Kelsey's moans grew louder. Her fingers dug into the rug while she remained still. Mythia's tongue swirled around the exit before pressing her tongue to it, imagining invading it with a few of her cocks.

"Rub your clit," Mythia ordered. She would allow this because she was following orders so perfectly.

Kelsey slid her hand between her opened legs and rubbed wide circles along her clit. The sound of her wetness filled the room.

Her breathless moans were growing louder.

Mythia lifted her head and dropped a fair amount of spit onto Kelsey's dark hole. She rubbed it around the rim and pressed against it. The little muscle gave resistance at first before opening slightly. It was all she needed to slip her single finger inside. Kelsey's muscles clamped down around her.

It was a glorious sight to behold. She added a little more spit and pressed another finger in with the first one, and began to fuck her mate slowly. Her fingers were soon sliding in and out a little easier.

"Ahhh..." Kelsey cried, her fingers moving faster.

"Stop," Mythia ordered, keeping her fingers deep inside of Kelsey while batting her hand away with her free hand. "I said no orgasm until I said so."

Kelsey whimpered, her body trembling.

"You almost broke my rule."

"I'm sorry," Kelsey whispered, her face remaining pressed into the rug. She brought her hand up to join the other one, holding onto the rug as if her life depended on it.

Mythia withdrew her fingers and spread Kelsey's ass as wide as it could go. She licked Kelsey's entire pussy from her clit, back to her puckered rim.

"Hmm..." she groaned as she licked and consumed her mate's pussy. Her face was buried far into her mate's delicious cunt. The taste of it was meant for her. It was an aphrodisiac, and she would forever want to consume it.

"Yes," Kelsey sobbed, her body shaking violently the longer Mythia took eating what was rightfully hers.

Mythia sat back, her face coated with her mate's juices. Kelsey's pussy was so wet, Mythia could feel the trail of her cream running down her chin.

Turning Kelsey over, Mythia jerked her hips to where Kelsey straddled her.

She brought Kelsey's face to hers and claimed her lips again. Kelsey folded her arms around Mythia's neck and dove into the kiss.

Mythia filled her hands with Kelsey's ass and brought her flush to her, using her strength to move her mate against her.

Her pussy was flush against Mythia's stomach. She wanted her mate's cream all over her, as if to mark her. Kelsey thrust her hips, falling in line with Mythia's rhythm. She ground herself against Mythia without breaking the kiss.

Her gasps and moans were all captured by Mythia's mouth. Their breasts were crushed between them, their nipples rubbing together, creating a wonderful sensation.

Kelsey began thrusting faster, and Mythia gripped her tight in her arms.

"What did I say?" Mythia tore her lips

from Kelsey's. Tears swelled up in her mate's eyes and threatened to fall.

"Please," Kelsey whispered.

"Not until I say so."

Mythia slid her arms underneath Kelsey's legs and leaned forward. She rolled Kelsey far onto her back, where her legs were up in the air. Mythia rested on her knees and allowed Kelsey's bottom to lie on her chest.

This was a vulnerable position that put Kelsey's pussy right in her face. Her legs fell open, exposing everything. Mythia wrapped her arms around Kelsey's stomach to keep her in place.

"You were a bad girl, thinking you could waltz into my castle and steal from me." She rested her chin on Kelsey's bottom, the scent of her core like a drug. It was hard for her to concentrate on what she was thinking.

"I'm sorry," Kelsey whimpered.

"Are you?" She leaned forward and took a swipe of Kelsey's slit with her tongue. Kelsey's moans increased Mythia's need to claim her. She fought down the urge to bite her, to claim her.

"No, not really."

"I didn't think so." She began to tease

Kelsey more. This time, she pressed her tongue into her opening. The warmth of her core was a welcoming sensation. Mythia reached up and pressed a finger to Kelsey's clit.

Tears streamed Kelsey's face. Her moans were mixed with incoherent words as Mythia's finger began to quicken.

"Please," she gasped, her hips thrusting forward to meet Mythia's tongue.

Mythia paused again.

Kelsey cried out, her arms stretched out with her fists clinging to the rug. Her breasts shook from the sobs.

"I'm sorry. I won't come back again."

"Who said you get to leave?" Mythia slipped her tongue back inside. This time, she pressed it as far as it would go while applying more pressure to Kelsey's bundle of nerves. "I already said you belong to me."

She removed her hand and mouth from Kelsey.

"Oh, God," Kelsey cried, shuddering.

"Tell me you belong to me. I want to hear it." Mythia realized she was pushing her little human, but there was something about her, and she was not going to let her go tonight.

Not ever.

In the morning, she would explain about the mating.

Now, she had more pressing things on her hands.

"Do you want your orgasm?"

"Yes!" Kelsey screamed frantically. Her body shook as her wide eyes bore into Mythia's. Her body was covered with a fine sheen of sweat. Some of her hair was plastered to her face, while the rest was a tangled mess. She looked absolutely beautiful. "Please give it to me. Make me come."

Mythia thought of torturing her little human longer, but finally decided she'd had enough. One thing Kelsey was going to learn about being mated to a dragon shifter was that they had high libidos, and were very sexual in nature.

"Fine."

Mythia began to rub Kelsey's clit harder as she thrust her tongue back inside, fucking Kelsey with it.

Over and over, she sunk her tongue into the depths of her pussy while tantalizing her sensitive bud. Mythia pinched her clit and pulled on it.

Kelsey's muscles grew taut, and she finally detonated.

Her back arched off the floor as a scream erupted from her lips. She shook as the waves of her climax washed over her.

Mythia covered her entire pussy with her mouth and drank in her release, lapping up all the creamy essence that poured out of her mate.

Kelsey's pleasure belonged to her.

This orgasm was a reward for how well she followed directions tonight.

Kelsey flopped back down on the floor, spent. Her muscles were loose, and a slight snore escaped her. Mythia took one long lick of her pussy before releasing her legs.

Crawling over her spent mate, she watched her, the flicker of light dancing along her creamy skin. She rubbed a finger along Kelsey's bottom lip, entranced by the direct contrast of their skin color.

The difference didn't bother Mythia at all. The fates had decided Kelsey was made for her, and that's all she needed.

Tenderness she had never known flowed through her. The urge to protect this woman was strong and overpowering. In her dragon heart, she knew this was love.

It was the shifter way.

One look was all it took, and her life was forever changed.

Mythia gathered Kelsey into her arms and closed her eyes, using her magic to whisk them off to her bedroom.

Kelsey could sleep for a short while.

Mythia was far from done with her.

CHAPTER FIVE

Kelsey's eyes flew open. She didn't know what woke her. Blinking, she tried to get her eyes to focus. Her gaze landed on a bed that wasn't hers.

"What the—"

She tried to move her hands, but they were locked in place, though there was nothing on her wrists.

Dammit.

The invisible handcuffs.

She had always heard that dragons had magic, but she'd never seen it in the works. Now she had firsthand knowledge.

Kelsey tried to look around as much as she could to take in where she was.

A bedroom.

The large, four poster bed could easily sleep four to five adults. The sheets underneath her were the finest she'd ever felt. They brushed against her skin, sending a shiver of desire down her spine.

"Oh, goodness." She briefly closed her eyes, trying to control the state of horniness she found herself in.

Boy, had she gotten herself into a world of trouble. She never in a million years would've thought her punishment for breaking into someone's home would result in being fucked by the owner.

The memories of Mythia dominating her came to mind, and her body immediately roared to life. She dropped her forehead to the mattress and groaned. She had never had this type of reaction to any of her lovers before.

Just a memory, and her pussy was begging to be fucked. She was still naked, and the cool air caressed her skin. Goosebumps formed along her arms and her ass.

Her core clenched with need. Moisture

seeped from her, coating her thighs. Her body was craving release.

What was wrong with her?

She'd had plenty of one-night stands with women she had just met, but there was something different with what transpired between her and Mythia.

She needed Mythia.

She wanted her to fuck her again.

Sex with the dragon one time, and she was already feeling like a strung-out crack addict. The orgasm she experienced was life-altering. She'd never been one to say she saw stars, but holy hell.

Not only did she see them, but she also flew amongst them.

"No. I have to get out of here." She didn't know what time it was, but she was sure it had to be past midnight. She just hoped and prayed Jasper had left like she'd ordered him to.

Kelsey tugged at her arms, but the hold on her tightened. She had to find a way to get out of here. She was sure Jasper was going crazy.

Her hair fell forward onto her face. She

blew the strands away, but they just fell back into place.

How the hell could she break free from handcuffs she couldn't even see?

She'd have to figure out a way, then find her clothing. Or maybe take the sheet of the bedding so she could break out of there. She'd managed to slip into the castle, and she would manage to find a way to get out.

Kelsey tugged again, but her restraints tightened more.

Dammit.

"You're finally awake."

Kelsey froze in place. She knew without looking who stood near her. She could sense Mythia. She didn't know how, but she could pinpoint where she stood in the room.

"Why are you holding me captive? Didn't you get what you wanted from me?" Kelsey asked.

Mythia's chuckle sounded behind her.

"You don't get to ask me questions." The bed dipped down as Mythia crawled over to her, stopping at Kelsey's side. Moving Kelsey's hair away from her face, a devilish grin spread across Mythia's lips. "But I will grant you one, and I'll even provide it for you."

Kelsey swallowed hard. Mythia's amber eyes practically glowed as she stared at her.

"What question—"

"I will provide you the question you are to ask me," Mythia interjected sternly.

Kelsey's mouth slammed shut. She inhaled sharply and took in the naked dragon shifter lying next to her. Her brown skin was flawless. Kelsey's fingers itched to run along it to see if it was as soft as she imagined it to be.

"Okay," Kelsey breathed. She was mesmerized by the amber orbs locked on her. Whatever spell this woman was weaving over her, she was falling for it.

"Now repeat after me. How are you going to fuck me this time?" Mythia reached over and tucked the hair that threatened to fall forward again behind Kelsey's ear.

Kelsey blinked.

Mythia wasn't done with her.

She bit her lip and tried to resist fidgeting. The urge to spread her legs and beg for another orgasm was rising.

Pressing a kiss to her shoulder, Mythia rested a hand on the small of Kelsey's back.

"Ask the question," Mythia said again, raising an eyebrow while she waited.

"How..." Kelsey hesitated at first. The burning desire in Mythia's eyes caused her breath to catch. She cleared her throat and continued. "How are you going to fuck me this time?"

"I'm so glad you asked, mate." Mythia shifted on the bed and braced herself over Kelsey. Tugging Kelsey's head to the side to expose her neck, she pressed her face into the crook of Kelsey's shoulder and inhaled deeply.

Kelsey closed her eyes, basking in the sensation of Mythia pressing hot, open-mouthed kisses along her spine.

Kelsey's eyes suddenly flew open. "Wait, what did you just call me?"

She didn't hear her like she thought she did.

There was no way that she called her—

"Mate?" Mythia stopped at the swell of Kelsey's ass.

"Why would you call me that?"

"Because that is what you are to me,"

Mythia answered matter-of-factly, while using her knees to spread Kelsey's thighs apart.

"But I can't be." How could she be the mate of a dragon? Her heart raced so fast, she was afraid she was going to faint.

It would explain Mythia's possessive nature the moment they met. Was it true that it only took one look for them to recognize their mates? She'd heard it was similar for wolf shifters.

From what she had heard, mating was for life.

But she wasn't a dragon shifter. She was human.

"But how do I know you speak the truth?" Her body jerked from a sharp pain on her ass. She cried out and glanced over her shoulder.

Mythia had bitten her.

"We're going to have to teach you how to remain obedient," Mythia muttered. "You know you feel it deep down inside of you. I could tell the moment I looked you in the eyes, you felt the connection between us. The urge. The need. The desire to mate."

Kelsey lowered her head to the bed.

Was Mythia right?

Were all those feelings fate telling her she belonged to Mythia? That they were to be with each other for all eternity?

She may be human, but she kept up with the latest information from her shifter friends. She knew how matings worked.

"You felt all that, didn't you?" Mythia asked softly, caressing the swell of Kelsey's ass.

There was no use lying.

Shifters would be able to scent it.

"Yes." It was true. She had felt all of that when Mythia appeared before her in the library.

A spark appeared in her heart, as if acknowledging the bond unlocking something inside of her. Warmth spread through her chest.

Or was it desire?

Mythia's hand and mouth were too dangerous. She couldn't think right now.

"Get up on your knees," Mythia ordered, her voice husky with lust.

Kelsey pushed up onto her knees, and the restraints on her wrists slightly eased, allowing her to rest on all fours.

"Very good girl." Mythia's hand ran along her rim and down to her pussy. Her fingers dove into her slick slit. "Look how wet you've become."

Kelsey groaned while Mythia dragged some of her wetness to her anus. She licked her lips, her body tensing in anticipation. She spread her legs wider, sensing she was going to enjoy whatever Mythia was going to do to her.

Not once had Mythia caused her any pain.

"Look at how you're presenting yourself to me." A warm substance coated her dark hole, and Mythia's finger slowly rubbed it in. Kelsey bit back a moan and fought to hold still. She wasn't sure if she wanted Mythia to add to her punishment. "You shall be rewarded for having a wet cunt and a sexy ass."

* * *

Mythia knelt behind her beautiful mate. To hear Kelsey confirm she had sensed the mating bond had Mythia wanting to push her over and sink her teeth into her to claim her.

Soon, she promised her dragon.

Her animal was impatient. Especially now that their mate was in their grasp.

She waved her hand, and her favorite strap-on appeared in place on her body. She glanced down beside her knee and found another thick dildo she planned to use on her mate.

One of her goals in life would be to bring Kelsey immense pleasure. There was nothing that would please her more than to watch her mate fall apart during their lovemaking.

"Before I claim you,"—Mythia rested her finger along Kelsey's puckered rim—"I will take you here first."

"Oh, God." Kelsey's whisper didn't go unnoticed. Mythia's sensitive hearing was able to pick up the faintest of sounds.

"No, Kelsey. I'm just your mate," Mythia chuckled. What they were about to do had nothing to do with any gods. "It will be my job to forever take care of you and provide everything you should ever need. Tonight, you need me. I can sense it."

She conjured more of the clear lubricant onto Kelsey's ass. She didn't want her mate to experience any pain.

Only pleasure.

"You are not to come until I tell you to," Mythia instructed. Her ears picked up on the slight sound of Kelsey's sharp intake of breath. Soon, Kelsey would learn that Mythia knew what was best for her, and that if she was a good girl, she would be rewarded with more pleasure than she could tolerate. "Do you understand me, love?"

"Yes." There was no hesitation this time with her response.

Mythia smiled.

Her mate was learning.

She lined up the blunt tip of the cock attached to her waist and pushed forward, sinking it deep inside of Kelsey with one thrust.

"Oh, it's so big," Kelsey groaned. Her hips bucked around as if to accommodate it. Mythia eyed the sight of her channel stretching around the thick width of the cock. All the toys Mythia kept on hand were oversized and meant for extreme pleasure.

She moved her thumb and began massaging Kelsey's dark hole.

"Are you in pain?" she asked.

Kelsey shook her head.

"Don't move unless I tell you to," Mythia commanded, snagging Kelsey's hair to anchor her. "Are you going to move?"

"No." Her breathless answer was all Mythia needed to hear. She withdrew slightly, leaving the tip inside of Kelsey before pushing forth again.

Kelsey's fingers dug into the mattress.

Mythia tugged on Kelsey's hair, causing her to arch her neck back. She rested on all fours and looked magnificent. Her breaths were shallow, while her low whimpers caused Mythia's beast to prowl around.

Mythia began with slow, rhythmic strokes.

Kelsey was the perfect mate, remaining still as she was instructed. Mythia picked up her pace, sinking her cock in deep and hard.

Kelsey's pleasure spilled from her lips in cries, chants, and incomprehensible words.

"Mythia," she called out. Her muscles grew tense, and Mythia paused in her thrusts, leaving the cock fully wedged inside of her.

Mythia rubbed her ass with her free hand. She looked forward to the future and all the years she would have with this woman.

She released Kelsey's hair. "You're being such a good girl, following my orders." She ran her hand along the curve of Kelsey's spine until she came to her waist. She gripped both sides of her hips and withdrew slightly. The cock glistened, covered in Kelsey's cream.

Her mate was thoroughly enjoying being fucked from behind.

Mythia tucked that little bit of information into the back of her mind for future reference.

"Do you want more?" Mythia asked, slowing sliding the cock back inside of her cunt. Kelsey's breaths began to calm down. A moan escaped her, but she didn't respond to Mythia. "Kelsey. Do you want more?"

"Yes." Her breathless answer was barely audible.

Mythia reached for the second dildo that rested on the bed. It was a thick cock with fake balls that would help her keep a good hold on it while she fucked her mate. She ensured there was plenty of warm, clear gel on Kelsey's rim. Pressing the head of the dildo to her puckered entrance, the other cock stayed nestled inside of her pussy.

Her anus resisted the cock at first, but Mythia was able to work the tip inside.

A deep groan rumbled from Kelsey while Mythia advanced the dildo inch by inch inside of her tight hole. The sight of her anus opening and accepting the thick dick was extremely arousing. Mythia moaned, watching her mate be filled. Once it was lodged in completely to its fake balls, she paused.

She was in love with her mate.

Fate had chosen the perfect woman for her.

"My love, I wish you could see what I see. I want you to appreciate what I'm doing for you."

"God, I do."

"That's good. You'll show me how much later." Mythia brought out the hand cock and pushed it back in a slow rhythm. Her ass was clutching the cock as if it didn't want to let it go. She continued to fuck her mate, rocking her hips forward in tandem with her hand's movement.

Kelsey cried out.

Mythia couldn't take her eyes off the sight of her mate taking both of the cocks.

Kelsey became more vocal, her cries echoing through the air. Her body trembled, her head falling forward.

"You're doing so well, Kelsey, my love." The gushy sounds of her juices kept distracting Mythia. She wanted to lean down and lick it all off her mate. Her taste was addictive, and she needed to have every drop on her tongue.

Pausing her movements, she took Kelsey in. Her mate was close, and by the looks of her, she was trying her damnest to not climax.

"It's time for your reward," Mythia announced. "You have permission to move. Take your pleasure and your release, my dear."

Kelsey shuddered and rocked her hips forward before pressing back into Mythia.

"Oh, shit!" Her hips began moving faster as she fell back on both cocks.

Mythia used her dragon's magic to hold the anal cock in place. She gripped Kelsey's hips and helped guide her back.

"Yes... yes..." Kelsey chanted and began

to sob while her body trembled. She threw her head back and screamed, "I can't! I can't take it!"

"You can," Mythia growled around her descended fangs. She pumped her hips, helping the cock reach the deepest part of Kelsey's pussy.

Kelsey dropped down onto her elbows, putting her ass even higher in the air. Mythia took over and began to thrust both cocks into her mate, and she took her hard.

Kelsey grew tense, her fingers clutching the sheets into her tight fists. Another scream erupted from her as she came again.

Mythia growled and withdrew the cocks. Kelsey's body relaxed down on the bed, her panting heavily.

With a swipe of her hand, the strap-on vanished and reappeared on the nightstand. Mythia crawled over Kelsey and balanced over her while she laid facedown on the mattress.

Her mate was spent. Mythia was pleased at how much pleasure she gave her. She wasn't worried about hers at the moment. They had a lifetime for Kelsey to learn how to please her, and the lessons would start tomorrow.

Mythia pressed a gentle kiss on the nape of Kelsey's neck. Brushing the hair away from her face, she then kissed her cheek.

"Rest now, mate."

CHAPTER SIX

Kelsey opened her eyes and took in her surroundings.

"So last night wasn't a dream." She sat up in the bed and brought the blankets up to cover her naked form. There was no sign of Mythia. She was uncertain if this was Mythia's bedroom. From the looks of it, it probably was.

The room was massive, and was decorated in warm colors, the large bed being the centerpiece. There was a sitting area in front of a fireplace that had a hearth so large, she was sure she could stand up straight in it. It reminded her of the medieval times, but then remembered the castle had been built centuries ago.

Now that she really took everything in, she noticed the updated technology. There was a flatscreen television sitting on a stand near the couches. There were hardwood floors and floor-to-ceiling windows with thick drapes adorning them.

A knock sounded at the door.

Kelsey gripped the blanket in front of her.

"Come in," she called out. Her heart quickened, but then she realized Mythia wouldn't knock on the door. She owned the place.

The door opened, and a woman with long black hair stepped inside. She was dressed in a black skirt and white shirt, covered by an apron.

"Good morning, my lady," she greeted, giving a deep curtsey. "My name is Antha. I assume you slept well?"

"Morning. Yes, I did." Kelsey's cheeks grew warm. Did this woman know the mistress of the house had screwed her until she barely had a voice left? She swallowed hard and grimaced at how hoarse her voice was when speaking.

Every orgasm Mythia gave her ended in her screaming to the high heavens.

She'd never been fucked like that before.

Kelsey reached up and tucked her hair behind her ear.

"Good. I was instructed to assist you this morning." She held up a robe as she made her way over to the bed and waited for Kelsey.

Kelsey slid across the bed, trying to keep the blankets close to her. Standing, she dropped the blanket and quickly placed her arms in the sleeves and wrapped it around her body.

"Thank you."

"My pleasure. Please, follow me, my lady." Antha spun around on her heel and walked swiftly over to a door near the bed.

Kelsey followed her in and paused in the doorway. Her eyes grew wide at the size of the bathroom.

It was larger than her apartment.

Marble floors, dark wood double vanities, and a porcelain soaking tub with a walk-in shower next to it. There was even a chaise and side table along the wall.

It was like standing inside a luxury hotel bathroom.

"A bath or a shower?" Antha asked. Opening a drawer to one of the vanities, she placed toiletries on the granite countertop.

"A shower will be fine." Kelsey had never had someone wait on her before. It was hard not to dismiss the woman.

She could prepare her own shower.

But since she said she was instructed, Kelsey would leave well enough alone. She didn't want to get the woman into trouble.

So she sat patiently and waited for Antha to let her know when it was time to enter the shower.

"The shower is ready for you. I will bring you a change of clothes to wear." Antha moved over to the door. "If you find you need anything else, press that button right there." Antha pointed to a display on the wall near the door.

"Thank you." Kelsey stood up and waited for the door to shut. Once Antha was gone, she began to explore the room. The drawers held everything a person would need. Different shower gels, lotions, make-up, and hair supplies. "This place is amazing."

She dropped her robe and scurried over to the shower. The water was warm and felt so good against her sore muscles. Her body felt as if she had worked out. Kelsey stood under the spray of water and allowed it to flow all along her body.

Her gaze landed on the shower gel, shampoo, and conditioner Antha had placed on the shelf.

She took her time washing herself and her hair. Her shower at home had nothing on this one. She didn't want to leave.

Once she was finished, she stepped out of the shower and reached for the towels hanging nearby, using one to wrap around her, and another to wrap around her wet hair.

Padding over to the vanity, she stared at herself in the mirror.

"Who are you?" she whispered. She had come to this castle with the intent of retrieving her family's heirloom. But instead, she'd gotten way more than she bargained for.

Multiple orgasms, and the knowledge she was the mate of the mistress of the castle.

How was it possible she was able to sense Mythia and the connection between them?

She knew a few mixed species couples, and none of the humans had felt the mating bond.

What was special about her?

Kelsey closed her eyes and inhaled. Now that Mythia wasn't near her, she could finally think clearly.

She was going to have to speak with Mythia and explain exactly why she came to the castle. She needed that necklace. She wasn't leaving here without it.

After she finished blow drying her hair, she went into the bedroom. On the bed were clothes, just as Antha had promised. A black lace bra, a matching thong, and a long maxi dress with three quarter length sleeves. The dress was the same color as the lingerie.

She shrugged her shoulders and put them on. Surprisingly, they were the correct sizes.

"How did they know?" She spun around at the sound of the door opening and watched Mythia step into the room.

She exuded power and sex appeal. Her long dark hair was plaited into intricate braids and rested along her shoulders. She was dressed in a navy tunic and leather pants with high-heeled boots.

"Good morning, mate." Mythia stopped in front of her. Her amber eyes glowed, even in the daylight. She cupped Kelsey's cheeks and pressed her lips to hers.

Kelsey was unable to resist the kiss. She leaned into the shifter and opened her mouth. The kiss brought her body to life. Her hands slid up to rest at the base of Mythia's neck. The kiss grew deeper until Mythia broke away from her. She grinned and ran her thumb along Kelsey's bottom lip.

"Morning," Kelsey breathed, her core pulsating with need.

Down, hussy.

Kelsey tried to get control of her body. Again, the second Mythia was near her, she practically went up in flames. The need to be consumed by this dragon shifter was growing. She was painfully aroused by just a kiss.

"I'm told breakfast is ready for us." Mythia ran her hands along Kelsey's arms. "I need to feed you. We burned plenty of energy last night."

Kelsey froze in place.

Not once did Mythia ask for anything from her. She could have demanded she returned any and all favors, but she hadn't.

Kelsey felt absolutely horrible. Never had she been so selfish when it came to sex. She had been so caught up in the pleasure Mythia was giving her, she didn't think that Mythia had not gotten her own release.

"What's wrong, my love?" She entwined their hands together and brought them up to her lips. She pressed a soft kiss to the back of it.

"Last night, I didn't, um..." She didn't know what to say exactly that wouldn't sound crude. She had gotten a quick taste of Mythia's pussy, and it was the sweetest pussy she'd ever tasted.

"Give me an orgasm?" Mythia grinned before pressing another hard kiss to Kelsey's lips. "Don't worry, my love. We have a dragon's lifetime for you to make me climax. Last night was all about you. Bringing you pleasure gave me pleasure."

"But—"

"No buts." Mythia placed a finger on Kelsey's lips, then removed it and stepped back, pulling on Kelsey's hand. "Come. I'm sure breakfast will be fit for a queen. My servants have been made fully aware that you are my mate."

She released Kelsey's hand and stalked over to the door.

"I did come here to steal from you," Kelsey blurted out. It took just that small distance for her to have a clear mind again.

Mythia paused. She didn't turn around or say a word. Kelsey grew nervous and eyed the door. If she needed to make a run for it, there was no way she would be able to get past Mythia.

"Is that so?" Mythia turned around and narrowed her gaze on Kelsey.

She swallowed hard and automatically took a step back. The air in the room had suddenly dropped a few degrees. Maybe she shouldn't have said anything.

"Yes."

Mythia ambled over to her, the muscles in her jaw ticking. She stopped in front of Kelsey and studied her.

"What were you going to steal?" Her low,

calm voice was quite frightening. "Was it in the reading room?"

Kelsey nodded once.

Mythia wrapped her arm around her and brought her flush to her. The room they were in vanished before her, and seconds later, they were back in the reading room.

"Show me.

* * *

Mythia released her hold on Kelsey. Anger filled her at the thought that she had been correct. She had tried to forget and not focus on the reason for her mate coming to be in her home.

I did come here to steal from you.

Kelsey's voice echoed in her head. Her dragon blew out a deep breath and prowled around. She wanted to transport to the roof and shift to let her animal take over.

Her dragon was ready to hunt something down and kill it.

With wide eyes, Kelsey took a step back, away from Mythia.

Mythia didn't like the faint scent of fear coming from her mate. She would assure her mate that even though she was pissed, she would never do her harm. But first, she needed to see what it was she came to take.

Mythia folded her arms in front of her and watched Kelsey walk around the room. She went back to the exact spot she was in when Mythia barged into the room. Kelsey faced a shelf and stared at the object sitting before her.

Mythia went to stand beside her.

"This," Kelsey whispered.

"The Rose medallion?" Mythia froze in place. The memory of the night she'd won it off her friend came to mind. Paxton had lost to her in a fair game of cards. Their stakes had been high, but unfortunately for him, he paid the price. He was a man of his word and gave the medallion to her as pay- ment. "What could you possibly want with that?"

Aside from its worth, why would she risk breaking into the castle to steal it?

Did her mate need money?

Mythia growled. She would pay all her mate's debts. Her woman would never want for anything ever again. The vault was not too far from them, and soon, she would present her hoard to Kelsey. First, they needed to deal with the matter at hand.

"It belongs to my family." Kelsey stared at the medallion with such admiration, tears rested on the tips of her eyelashes. "It was stolen from my family, and we—"

"I do not steal," Mythia interjected. She took Kelsey by the arm and forced her to face her. "That medallion is mine. Whatever tale you've heard surrounding this medallion is false."

"My grandfather wouldn't lie to my mother." Kelsey shook her head fiercely and snatched her arm back. "It belongs to my family, and I will take it back."

She snatched the medallion off its post and gripped it close to her.

Mythia was hit with a strong sense of a dragon roaring off in the distance.

This was her territory, and no one should be invading it. The ground shook with a power that caused them to stumble.

"What is this?" Mythia growled. She was suddenly hit with a wave of power radiating from Kelsey.

"What's going on?" Kelsey cried out, dropping the medallion as if it were too hot to hold. It bounced around on the floor before landing at Mythia's feet. She pressed her hands to her chest and grimaced in pain.

The rocking of the building ceased.

"Let me see your hands." Mythia took them into hers and carefully studied them. The redness of her palms was starting to fade before her eyes. She glanced down at the necklace. Was it warded against certain people? Why would it try to harm her mate?

And who the hell did it?

"What the hell just happened?" Kelsey asked. The scent of her fear was growing, and it sent Mythia's dragon into a frenzy.

"I don't know, but I'll soon find out," Mythia replied through clenched teeth. Her dragon sensed the other one headed toward her castle. It was moving fast and getting closer.

She would need to go out and meet this dragon.

Picking up the medallion, Mythia held it in her hands. It'd been a while since she had, and she'd never had a reaction like Kelsey just had.

She reached over for the velvet material it had sat upon. Wrapping it up, she handed it back to Kelsey. She would have to have Sascha come explain what the hell had just happened.

"What are you doing?" Kelsey cried out.

"Take it. I want you to go back to my room and stay." Mythia wrapped her arm around Kelsey and brought her flush against her. She instantly transported them back to her bedroom. The room was warded against the strongest magic, and would keep her mate safe.

They reappeared in the master bedroom.

"Don't leave this room." Mythia spun around and marched to the door, sending a quick telepathic message to Sascha. This was urgent. There was no time to wait for the reply.

"Where are you going?"

"You will be safe here. My seer will come for you." Mythia backed away from her mate before leaving the room. Once in the hall, she closed her eyes and vanished.

CHAPTER SEVEN

Mythia stood on her landing. Wisps of her hair broke free from her braids and whipped around from the strong gusts of wind.

She walked forward, taking in the rolling clouds. The sky had grown angry. Where the sun was perched high with its warm rays shining down on the town of Saxon Hills, now appeared as if a storm was racing toward them.

Only it wasn't a storm.

It was a dragon in *her* territory.

She looked around at the spacious landing pad on the top of the castle. It was perfect for departures and arrivals when in her beast form.

Mythia looked east, feeling the other beast getting closer.

Mythia gave into her animal and allowed her to break free. Her clothes fell away in tattered shards. Her magic swirled around her as her beast grew to its massive size of seventy-five feet long.

Onyx, leathery scales thick as armor covered her body. Her massive talons scraped along the concrete of the landing with her first steps. She stretched out her wide wings and threw her head back. A deep roar flew from her mouth to warn the incoming intruder.

Mythia jumped up into the air, her wings carrying her in the direction she sensed the other dragon. She cut swiftly through the wind, flying higher into the thick clouds.

This was her territory, and no one had the right to invade it. For hundreds of years, she'd protected it as a promise to a good friend. Now she had even more reason to ensure Saxon Hills remained safe.

Her mate was there.

She glided through the darkened sky in

search of him.

A screeching roar sounded.

He was close.

She recognized the call of the other dragon.

Xomor.

He was an older dragon she was very familiar with. She'd met him in battle almost a century ago, defending her territory.

She'd kicked his ass and sent him packing with the threat if he ever returned, she'd do it again.

The clouds parted, and her gaze landed on the blue dragon that shot through the air, headed straight toward her.

You don't belong here! she roared through the mental link all dragons shared. It was a form of communication when in their animal forms. *I warned you before.*

You don't rule me, girl, he retorted as he flew closer to her, his talons braced for attack.

She spat a line of fire toward him. He dodged it, turning on his side and flying in another direction.

This area is mine, she growled. Her beast was pissed that another dragon was within miles of her mate. She swiftly dove after him, following him as he headed toward a mountainous range.

Their speed was faster than any airborne animal, cutting through miles within minutes.

The coward thought he would run from her? She would ensure he never returned again. She picked up speed, gaining on him, her dragon's fire spewing from her open jaws.

Xomor cut left and dove lower toward the rocky edges of the mountain. She followed close by, twisting and turning her large body while avoiding slamming into a wall of rocks.

She cursed and pulled up higher.

He was crazy to fly so low and close to the jagged earth.

Her eyes trailed him as he went higher until he came to a leveled area and landed. She flew around in wide circles overhead, unsure of what he was doing. She eyed him warily.

Come down and meet me. We can talk in our human forms! he called out.

I'm supposed to trust you? She snorted. Her beast growled, not at all trusting the blue dragon. What business would he have to discuss with her?

Her curiosity was piqued. The human side of her wanted to hear him out, while the dragon side of her wanted to destroy him.

Xomor thew his head back and roared. The surrounding air swirled as he transitioned back to his human form. He stood tall with his hands in the air, as if to show he wasn't a threat.

That was a joke.

He was an old and powerful dragon shifter.

Mythia circled around one last time before descending. The ground shook from the weight of her animal hitting it. She pulled back on her animal, who gave her resistance.

Her beast wasn't as nice as she was.

After a battle of wills, her animal finally relented and gave her control of their body again. She transitioned swiftly and reappeared in her human form.

She wasn't a dummy and had summoned her weapons. She was dressed in her warrior leathers and had her favorite daggers sheathed at her waist.

Mythia stalked forward, narrowing her gaze on the man. He was tall and broad shouldered. His muscular figure was dressed in a silver tone metal link armor shirt, leather pants, and dark boots. He too had conjured his weapons. A broad sword was visible over the top of his head. He had a hard jawline that was clenched, a crooked nose, and dark, piercing eyes.

"What do you want?" she demanded. There was no point in drawing out the purpose of this meeting. This wasn't a personal visit. He needed to state his business and leave.

"Always like you to be so forward," he snapped.

She stopped yards away and eyed him. He had a foot in height on her, and about fifty pounds, but she didn't let that intimidate her. She was a seasoned warrior who had fought in her share of wars over her lifetime.

"And like I said before, if I see you in my territory again, I'll kill you." Her hand slid down to rest on the hilt of her dagger. She would be only too happy to carry out her promise. "What the fuck do you want?"

"You young dragons are so impatient." He began to pace. She watched him, tightening her hand on the hilt. "There was an explosive amount of energy released here recently."

Chills rolled down her spine. That wasn't too long ago. Had he already been near and she had been too caught up with her mate to notice another dragon was nearby?

"It's no concern of yours. I'll handle it," she replied. There was no reason for her to try to lie, since he would pick it up.

"It is very much my concern. Someone touched the medallion recently," he stated matter-of-factly.

She kept her face void of any expression. Her dragon didn't like the fact he knew of something that had happened deep in her castle.

"I see you aren't going to confirm, but I don't need you to." Xomor's lip raised in a sneer, the cocky son of a bitch. He knew something she didn't, and it pissed her the fuck off. "That medallion was cursed centuries ago. I'm bound to it."

She froze in place. That couldn't be. She won it off her friend Paxton years ago. She would have known if there was magic on that damn necklace. She would have sensed it.

"You lie," she hissed.

"Believe what you want, but I'm telling you, I need to know who it was that touched it." His smile vanished. His eyes darkened as a growl rumbled from his chest.

"Who would bind you to something that doesn't belong to you?" she snapped. Her anger was rising. There was no way in the seven hells she would reveal who had touched the necklace.

Xomor would never come near her mate.

"Oh, see, that's where this gets really interesting. A witch bound me to it for a sense of protection for those who shall hold it in their possession—"

"I don't need protection." Her patience was wearing thin. She eyed the sky and found it was clearing up, the darkness fading to light. A few birds flew overhead, as if the bad storm had passed.

But there was a sense of dread in the pit of Mythia's stomach.

The storm was far from over.

It was just beginning.

"My binding is to my descendants, who shall hold the ruby medallion. You may have kept me from my many times removed grandson before, but this descendent you won't."

Kelsey?

He would never come near her. She was the only person who would protect Kelsey. She didn't need Xomor's help.

"We're done here." Mythia turned and stalked away from him.

"You can't keep me from them. I will find out, and I will come for my descendant," Xomor hollered behind her. She ignored his ranting, shifted back into her beast, and took off.

* * *

"Why am I sent away to wait in a room as if I'm a child?" Kelsey muttered. She paced back and forth in front of the hearth. Once Mythia had stormed out of the room, Kelsey placed the medallion, still wrapped in the velvet material, on the nightstand. She didn't know what else to do with it.

She just knew she didn't want to touch it again with her bare hands.

Her footsteps faltered at the sound of a

roar of a dragon. It was long and powerful, as if to warn something off.

Mythia.

Kelsey knew without even having to look. She could sense her dragon was near.

When did Mythia become *her* dragon?

When she fucked you into submission.

Sighing, she ran her fingers through her hair. The little voice in the back of her head was right.

I must be going crazy.

She was already missing Mythia. Did she believe in fate? That this crazy thing between them was predestined by a higher power?

Kelsey didn't have an answer. She only knew that she was drawn to Mythia, and the bond between them was growing stronger.

What was even crazier was that Mythia hadn't even officially claimed her yet.

Once she did, the pull between them would be magnified.

Kelsey glanced out the windows, seeing the darkness fall.

Wasn't it just morning? Mythia had said breakfast was waiting for them.

What was going on? It didn't take a rocket scientist to know that Mythia was pissed about something. Kelsey had so many unanswered questions.

She was unaware of how long she'd been in the room. Her bag hadn't been returned to her, so she had no way of being able to contact Jasper or her family.

"Oh, Jasper." She was going to have to find a way to let him know she was okay. Her mother and grandmother wouldn't worry. She sometimes picked up the night shifts for overtime, and could go a couple of days without speaking to them.

But Jasper, they spoke every single day.

She just hoped he wouldn't do anything crazy, like try to overtake the castle to rescue her.

"I've got to get out of here."

"Where would you go?"

Kelsey screamed. She spun around and found a tiny woman standing behind her. Her brown skin was flawless, with little to no wrinkles. Her silver hair was held back by two long braids.

"Who are you, and how are you so quiet?" Kelsey asked, holding her hand to her chest. Her heart was beating erratically from the surprise.

"My name is Sascha, and Mythia requested I see to you." The woman bowed her head as the maid had done. When she lifted her head, Kelsey could see her wise eyes. The woman was much older than she appeared.

"You're the seer?"

"I am. And no, I don't have the magical powers of teleportation."

Kelsey looked at the woman. If she didn't teleport in here, was she able to read her mind?

"Okay. Mythia said you would come for me."

"Yes. Please, walk with me." Sacha motioned for her to follow as she exited the room. It was the first time she'd seen any other parts of the upper levels of the castle.

Their footsteps echoed as they walked along in silence.

"Have you worked for Mythia long?" Kelsey asked.

"Yes, since I was a young girl."

They went down to the first level. The decor of the building was more modern than she would have expected. It was a mix of old and new. The woodwork throughout the castle was magnificent.

"You must be hungry, no?" Sascha inquired.

Kelsey was about to decline any offers of food until her stomach decided to answer for her.

"I guess I am." She rested a hand on her belly and followed Sasha into an oversized kitchen.

Her mouth dropped open in amazement. It was a chef's dream kitchen. It looked like a kitchen in a large restaurant. But then again, they were in a castle, and there were functions held here at least once a year. Though Kelsey had never been one to attend those lavish parties.

The aromas floating through the air enhanced her hunger pains.

"Fiona has made a wonderful breakfast for you." They ambled past an island to the back of the kitchen, to a small breakfast nook. A round table built into a bay window that showcased the lush land that surround the castle. Off in the distance, Kelsey could see the cliffs and open sky.

There was a pale woman sitting at the table, dressed in all black. Her long hair was as dark as midnight, and the black eyeliner surrounding her eyes made them appear even larger. She eyed Kelsey as she grew near.

"She's even more beautiful than you let on," the stranger spoke up.

"That wasn't of importance," Sascha replied. "Kelsey, this is Raven, a trusted ally of Mythia's. She is here to help you."

"What do I need help with?" She took a seat across from Raven. She sensed the woman was a witch. She'd met one or two before, and the energy radiating from her confirmed it. "I'm sorry. Why do I need the help of a witch?"

"Mythia sent me a message that there was something you touched that activated a strong energy source. Something you said belonged to your family." Sascha sat in the chair next to Kelsey, her voice was low and calm as she locked eyes with Kelsey.

"It does," Kelsey responded automatically.

A woman dressed in a chef's uniform entered the kitchen and waved from across the room. She must be Fiona.

"We can take you back in time to determine if you are telling the truth," Raven said.

"I am!" she exclaimed.

"We can do this after you eat or before," Raven remarked, shrugging.

"Wait." She held up her hands. "What do you mean, you can send me back in time? As in, time travel?" She had never heard of time travelers before.

"In a way. You can walk through periods of time as if you were there. It will seem very real, but no one will know you're there." Raven leaned forward and rested her elbows on the table.

Kelsey leaned back. The action of seeing the past was fascinating, and she was actually contemplating it.

"Will I get hurt? Are you sure they won't see me?"

"No, you won't get hurt. You are just re-visiting memories and bearing witness. You can't harm anything or offset the timeline of our dimension."

Kelsey glanced over at Fiona, who was putzing around near the stove.

"And this is something Mythia wants?" Was this why Mythia sent the seer to her? To show her the past and how she came to have the medallion?

"She only wants to show you the truth."

Sascha patted the top of Kelsey's hand. "Only with your own eyes will you believe her. She doesn't want anything to stand between the two of you."

Kelsey stared at them before jerking her head in a nod.

"Let's do it."

Raven pushed back from the table and walked around it, coming to a stop next to Kelsey. Her lips curved up in the corner in a crooked grin.

"We're doing this here?" Kelsey asked.

"Sure." She placed her fingers on Kelsey's forehead. "It doesn't matter where we are. This won't take long at all. Time in the past moves at a different pace."

Her pupils dilated until there was barely any white left in her eyes. The warmth of her fingers grew.

Kelsey's heart began to race.

"Don't be afraid," Sascha whispered. "Raven will pull you out at the right moment."

"Okay." The warmth continued down along her face and raced down her neck. Kelsey's eyes fluttered closed, and darkness took her.

CHAPTER EIGHT

Blinking, Kelsey found herself sitting at a table in a dark corner. She jerked back in the chair and looked around.

Holy shit.

She was in the past.

Raven had actually done it.

She took in the old saloon. She assumed it was the weekend with so many patrons present. She bit back a laugh. She expected Clint Eastwood to walk through the door dressed as a cowboy.

A rowdy bunch was crowded around the bar. Laughter filled the air, along with the sound of a piano playing. Tables were scattered around the room, with men drinking and playing cards. Waitresses bustled along, serving up drinks.

Her heart raced. She had always been intrigued about the past, but never thought she'd ever get to walk through it.

Kelsey's gaze landed on the wooden staircase that led up to the second level. She knew exactly what went on up there without even seeing the painted ladies leaning along the banister. Their wide smiles were seductive as they tried to entice gentlemen callers to their rooms.

Kelsey took in a familiar form that stepped out from one of the rooms.

Mythia.

She was dressed in a dark button-up shirt with the first two buttons undone, black pants, boots, and a set of red suspenders. Her hair was tousled and hanging down past her shoulders. She grinned as she walked past the women who appeared to be very familiar with her.

Kelsey tensed when two of the women tried to coerce her into going into a room with them.

Jealousy reared its ugly head. She wanted to race up the stairs and toss them all over the banister to get them away from her woman.

Her eyes widened.

Her woman?

She clenched her hands together to keep from bolting out of her chair.

This was before I was even born, she reminded herself.

Mythia finally broke away from the two.

"Maybe later, ladies. Someone important is waiting for me," Mythia told them as she jogged down the stairs.

Kelsey grew worried.

Mythia was a black woman in an establishment filled with white men, and from looks of their clothes, it had to be some time in the 1800s.

Kelsey looked down at herself and found her clothes were that of this time period. Raven had placed her in a pale dress. If they couldn't see her, why were her clothes changed? Knowing she couldn't get an answer, she turned her attention back to her dragon shifter.

Mythia strode down the stairs, confidently navigating her way through the saloon. She was headed toward a table across the room where a single man sat.

Kelsey needed to be closer.

There was a reason she was sent here.

Kelsey got to her feet. No one paid her any attention when she stepped away from her table and followed Mythia.

It amazed her that the men nodded and tipped their glasses to Mythia. There was nothing but respect in their expressions.

They must know she's a powerful dragon shifter who could annihilate the town in minutes.

She really wanted to explore the building. This was a once-in-a-lifetime opportunity, but she needed to see what Mythia wanted her to see.

Mythia threw back her head and laughed before taking the seat across from the man. When she was seated, she motioned for the waitress.

Kelsey made her way over. The man looked familiar, but she couldn't place him. She didn't know why, seeing as she didn't live in this time period and would never have met him.

"We need alcohol if we're going to celebrate," Mythia said. The waitress arrived with a bottle, two glasses, and a deck of cards.

"Here's your usual, sweetie." Smiling at Mythia, the waitress sat everything down on the table. Mythia reached into her pocket and pulled out some cash, tucked it into the woman's top, and gave her a wink. The waitress blew her a kiss and walked away with a heavy sway in her hips.

Kelsey's hands balled into fists.

Jealousy wasn't something she'd ever experienced before. Most of her relationships had been short and sweet. There were more one-night stands than actual relationships, but she'd never experienced emotions like this before.

The man laughed. "Don't think you can liquor me up so you can cheat." Picking up the deck of cards, he began shuffling them. "I know you shifters. You can drink all you want and not get drunk like us humans."

"What are you talking about?" Mythia took the bottle and filled their glasses. She didn't look as if she had aged one bit. "What are we wagering? Tonight may be too rich for your blood."

Mythia pulled some gold coins out of her pocket and set them down in the middle of the table. The man's eyes widened.

"Mythia, that's too much."

"What are you talking about? I can afford to bet them. I'm feeling confident that I won't lose them." Mythia's grin was cocky. She shrugged and motioned to the table. "You don't have to go high. This is a friendly game between friends. If I lose, and I won't, I'd rather lose to you."

He dealt their hands before reaching for his glass.

"That's some good damn whiskey."

"Nothing but the best for you, my friend." Mythia raised hers to him before she took another sip.

Mythia having a drink and playing cards with a friend. Was this what she was supposed to see? Kelsey took notice of a gentleman sitting a few tables away, who was openly staring at the two.

A shiver rippled down her spine at the intensity in his eyes. He was large and scary looking.

"Here's my wager." He reached inside of his jacket pocket and pulled out something familiar. Recognizing the ruby medallion, Kelsey gasped. Who was this man? Why was he gambling away her family heirloom?

So this was who stole it.

"There's been something I want to discuss with you," the man began, eyeing his cards before throwing one down.

"And that is?" Mythia rearranged her cards and looked at him. "This game would appear to be too rich for your blood. I feel an important request coming. A request I may not want to accept. They become costly."

Something passed between them, leaving Kelsey confused. The hairs on the back of her neck rose.

"There's a man sitting to my left." Pausing, he took another sip from his glass. When he placed it back on the table, she noticed his hand shook slightly. Swallowing hard, he focused on the table.

"The one in black with the long hair and crooked nose?" Mythia hadn't even turned her head. How did she know who he was speaking about? There were plenty of men in this establishment, and she had just described the scary man who was still staring at them.

"Yeah, that's the one. He's been following me around. I'm afraid for my life." He looked up and met Mythia's still gaze.

"You want me to take care of him?"

"Yes. I don't know what he wants, and I was thinking that the town needs a protector."

"And because I'm a dragon, you want it to be me?" Mythia threw out another card and leaned back in her chair. She was the epitome of sexy. Kelsey didn't miss the looks thrown Mythia's way. Some of the women, and even the men, appeared hopeful that they would gain her attention, but the dragon shifter was in a deep conversation with her friend. "Besides a nice expensive ruby medallion, why should I do this?

"Because a friend is asking. I need to make sure my people are safe."

They each threw out a card, then paused as they stared down at what was on the table.

"It would seem that I won," Mythia murmured and sat forward. "Are you sure you want to give it to me, Paxton?"

Kelsey felt as if she someone had punched her in the gut. Her eyes widened as she took in the features of the man that sat across from Mythia. Now she knew why he appeared so familiar.

Paxton Rose.

Her great-great-great-grandfather.

She slapped her hand over her mouth to keep from crying out. So the medallion hadn't been stolen. Mythia had won it from a friend in a card game. How had the story become so distorted through the years?

"Because of my respect for you and our friendship, I shall do this for you." Mythia reached across the table, gathered up her coins, and placed them in her pocked. She then grabbed the medallion and placed it around her neck.

Paxton's shoulders slumped in relief. "Thank you."

A roar sounded. Kelsey's eyes flew across the room and watched the scary man flip his table over. His face was contorted in anger as he headed toward them.

"Run, Paxton," Mythia ordered. Pushing back from the table, she got to her feet and faced the man.

Of course her dragon wouldn't run, even when a guy the size of an NFL lineman charges directly toward her.

Kelsey screamed as she watched him slam into Mythia with such force, he broke through the wall of the bar, crashing outside.

It was a full-fledged bar fight.

Kelsey ducked at a bottle that was thrown across the room and quickly made her way outside, holding the skirt of her dress up so she could step over the rubble without tripping.

She coughed, waving her hand in front of her face. The dust and debris from the busted wall floated through the air, but she was able to see the two circling each other.

"This is none of your concern, Mythia," the man growled.

"This is my town, and you're not welcome here," Mythia bit out through clenched teeth.

"Give me back the medallion." He darted for her, but Mythia was too fast for him. She blocked his hands and threw a punch, landing it squarely at his nose. The sound of bones breaking reached Kelsey's ears.

She stepped down from the landing of the bar next to where the horses were tied to the hitching post. The animals were fidgeting, obviously scared. Their eyes grew wide, and they began to pull back on the reins to free themselves.

Kelsey's attention turned back to Mythia, who landed a kick to the man's stomach.

"This is your last chance, Xomor. Leave," she warned.

"You think you can stop me? Think again." Turning, the man ran and leapt into the air. Kelsey's mouth dropped open as she watched him transform into a massive dragon. It was night, so she couldn't see what color he was. Mythia was pissed. Smoke was pouring from her nose. She took off running in the direction of Xomor and repeated the action.

Her dragon appeared and flew into the air.

Kelsey picked up her skirts and raced after them. She headed down the middle of the dirt road, ignoring the people running toward the saloon. Her eyes were on the two dragons flying in the sky.

The moon was full, and its rays shone down around her. She came to the edge of the small town and headed toward an open area of land.

She was mesmerized by the sight of the two dragons battling it out above her.

Fire lit up the sky. It was a beautiful sight to behold. Their fire lit up the darkness, showcasing the mountainous region and woods. The two large bodies crashed against each other, their talons clawing at each other mid-flight.

Kelsey was frozen in place. The male dragon was slightly larger than Mythia's, but her dragon was easily holding her own.

Who was this man?

She turned to look back at the town, not realizing how far away she had wandered. Where was Paxton? She had forgotten all about him once the man charged Mythia.

Her forehead began to feel warm in the center. She instantly recognized the touch.

"No. Not yet!" she yelled, but it was too late.

Everything went dark.

CHAPTER NINE

Mythia arrived at the landing of the castle. Dropping down, she forced her dragon to recede. She knelt on all fours and paused to get herself together.

How dare Xomor invade her territory. If it was war he wanted, then she would gladly meet him head-on. Standing, she conjured clothing to cover her body.

She stalked toward the entry of the castle. She needed to see her mate and ensure she was fine. Mythia had entrusted Sascha to take care of Kelsey while she was away.

Her mate needed to have absolute trust

in her, and the only way she would believe that Mythia did not steal her family heirloom would be for her to witness it herself.

She arrived at the door, flung it open, and stepped inside, taking the stairs down into the building. She sensed Kelsey's location.

The lingering trails of dark magic were in the air. Raven must have been successful in carrying out Mythia's request.

Closing her eyes, she teleported outside of the sunroom and inhaled deeply, trying to calm her animal down. Walking in, still charged from her flight and fight with Xomor, would scar Kelsey.

Mythia wanted to ensure that her mate had all her questions answered.

Exhaling, she entered the room.

Kelsey sat on the loveseat placed in front of the large window that overlooked the garden. Her feet were tucked underneath her as stared outside, looking deep in thought.

Sascha and Raven's conversation ceased when she walked across the room. She gave them a nod and headed straight to her mate.

Kelsey didn't hear her when she stopped and knelt down next to her. Mythia's beast grew worried.

"Kelsey, my love." Mythia rested her hand on Kelsey's knee. It was as if she were in a trance. Mythia looked over to Sascha and Raven for an answer, but they just shrugged. Sighing, she turned back to Kelsey. "Are you all right?"

Kelsey blinked and turned to her.

"Mythia," she breathed. Her gaze roamed over Mythia's body before returning to meet her eyes. "You're okay."

"Don't worry about me. I can take care of myself." Mythia took Kelsey's hand and gently stroked the back of it with her thumb.

"I saw everything." Kelsey turned away from Mythia, and her dragon didn't like it one bit. She held back a snarl, trying to push her back. "You were friends with Paxton Rose, my ancestor, who helped settle this town."

"He was a good friend of mine," Mythia confirmed.

"You won the medallion from him in a card game, so I guess I was in the wrong. Tales had been passed down in my family that it was stolen." Pulling her hand back, she reached up and tucked her thick hair behind her ear.

"You don't have to apologize for anything, mate. If I had thought something was stolen from me, I wouldn't rest until I retrieved it."

"There was a man in the saloon. You fought him that night..." Kelsey stopped and fiddled with her hands. Mythia waited patiently for her to continue. She remembered the night she'd won the medallion as if it were yesterday. She didn't want to mention Xomor, but she would when the time was right. She herself was still processing what he had shared with her. "Who was he?"

Mythia took Kelsey's hand again and entwined their fingers together. She wasn't going to lie to her mate. She would tell her the truth.

"His name is Xomor. He's a crazed dragon who challenged me."

"And did you win that night?"

"Of course I did." Mythia tilted her head back. Why would her mate ask if she won during a battle with another dragon? She may not be as old as Xomor, but she was a mighty dragon.

"I was worried when you were in the saloon and he came running at you," Kelsey chuckled, then fell into a fit of laughter. "He was twice your size."

"I have fought in many wars over my long life, and I can handle the largest of men. There is a modern saying I love: 'The bigger they are, the harder they fall.'"

Mythia felt Sascha and Raven's eyes on her. She turned and glanced over at them. Sascha stood and walked over to them.

"I need to speak with you for a moment," Sascha announced.

Something was wrong. The seer must have been picking up what had occurred between Xomor and her.

"Please excuse me." She leaned over and pressed a kiss to Kelsey's forehead. Standing, she walked with Sascha to the other side of the room, where Raven joined them.

"Mythia, there is something about your mate," Raven began, her black eyes intense. She was a powerful dark witch that Mythia trusted. She led the local coven, and had been at Mythia's side for a long while. There was no other witch that Mythia would allow to perform such magic on her mate. "I don't get the sense that she's fully human."

Mythia folded her arms across her chest and waited for her to continue.

"What I'm about to tell you must be kept in the utmost confidence."

Any information about her mate could be used against her. Until she had sealed the bond completely, the link between the two of them could be tested. She didn't want to chance Kelsey rejecting her claim.

"Yes, of course. You know you can confide in me."

"Me too, but I'm right, aren't I? She's more than what she appears," Raven murmured.

"Yes, and I don't think she knows. I felt the same when I first laid my eyes on her. I could instantly tell she sensed the bond between us. As we all know, humans are not susceptible to the mating bond like us." Mythia replayed Xomor's speech in her head. How the hell had a secret like that been kept from her mate? She quickly caught them up on her short battle with Xomor and their conversation. "Apparently, Xomor is her ancestor, and I don't think she's aware of a dragon link in her family."

"That is heavy shit." Raven's eyes grew wide. "Are you going to tell her?"

"Of course I am. He's claiming he is to protect his kinship who owns the medallion."

"That means you must claim her soon." Sascha gripped Mythia's arm. "He cannot go against the mating bond. But until then, he'll have a claim over his kin."

"He will not take her from me," Mythia bit out through clenched teeth. She held back a growl, not wanting to alert her mate that there was an issue. She would seal the bond with her mate tonight. Kelsey wouldn't be able to resist the call. The dragon's blood in her, no matter how minute, would answer the call.

"There's a disturbance coming." Sascha's eyes suddenly clouded over as a vision took her. She grew deathly still while the gods showed her what they wanted her to see.

Mythia's muscles tensed. Her beast grew quiet, waiting to hear what the seer was going to share with them.

Sascha jerked, blinking her eyes into focus and looking at Mythia.

"The humans. They are going to storm the castle," Sascha murmured.

"Why?" Mythia snapped. This was the last thing she needed. There wasn't going to be time to deal with the humans. Not with the threat of a dragon trying to take her mate away. Even though he had the right, being Kelsey's kin, she would still refuse to part with her mate.

"They're searching for her," Sascha replied.

They all turned and looked over at Kelsey, who was again staring out into the gardens.

"What did you see?" Mythia demanded. She needed to know how many humans they were talking about. If only a few, the castle security would deal with them.

"There is a man. One who she is very close with her," Sascha began.

"A lover?" Mythia growled.

She hadn't thought that her mate may have been in a relationship with another. Jealousy reared its ugly head. She was a possessive dragon, and the thought of any other person putting their hands on her mate in a sexual way was enough to make her see red. Her dragon roared. It wanted to fly high into the sky and release its blazing fire.

Sascha shook her head. "I'm not sure."

"Show me."

The seer placed her fingers on Mythia's forehead, and immediately Mythia was catapulted into the vision Sascha had been shown.

It was that of Kelsey and a handsome man drinking together at a bar. He had his arm wrapped around her shoulders while they drunkenly sung a song. The vision transitioned to another scene where they were in a factory, working alongside each other. The manner in which they touched each other revealed they were close. Elbowing each other, shoving playfully, laughing at something they shared. It could all be considered a form of flirting.

Was this man courting her woman?

Mythia was thrust back into the present.

"I will kill him," she sneered. Spinning on her heel, she marched over to Kelsey. She was so enraged, thinking that her mate was in a human relationship.

She would never want to know of past lovers her mate may have had. If she were to find out, she would go after them all and strike them down for just having touched her.

"Who is he?" Mythia demanded.

"Who is who?" Kelsey jumped and turned to face Mythia, her brown eyes wide.

"The man you're around all the time. I saw him in the seer's visions. He will come for you."

Kelsey sat forward. "Jasper?"

So the male had a name.

Jasper.

It was a weak, human sounding name. Whoever he was, he would not be taking her mate from the castle.

"You've heard from him?" Kelsey asked frantically. She pushed off the couch and stood before Mythia. "Please. I have to speak with him."

"You are not going to speak to him." Mythia took Kelsey by the arms and held her close. She would never let him near Kelsey. This woman was hers, and any relationships she'd had in the past would cease to exist. "Did you forget that you are my mate? You belong to me now. He cannot have you."

"It's not like that," Kelsey cried out. She

fought to free herself from Mythia's hold, but she tightened her grip.

"Then what is it like? I saw images of you and him together. He put his hands on you, and you allowed it. You laughed at his jokes, and you—"

"He's like a big brother to me!" Kelsey shouted, tears gliding down her cheeks. "We're best friends. There has never been anything between the two of us. He was here when I snuck into the building. I told him to leave if I didn't come back to him."

"What?"

Mythia released her. The sight of her tears was gut-wrenching. She hadn't meant to make Kelsey cry. The possessive nature of her being took over her body. She glanced down at Kelsey's arms, afraid she had hurt her.

"Jasper is the one person who has always had my back. We're friends, nothing more." Kelsey angrily wiped her face with her hands and looked at Sascha. "Did your visions show you anything other than us being friends? Did they show you we grew up together? Did they show you all the times I fucked other women?"

Kelsey took a step toward Sascha and Raven, but Mythia snuck a hand around her arm and pulled her back. Turning Kelsey to face her, Mythia reached up and cupped Kelsey's cheek.

"Do not be mad at her. It was I who made assumptions." She was an ass. Instead of just asking her mate calmly who the man was, she let her jealousy get the best of her. "I'm sorry."

Kelsey stared at her for a moment before looking away.

"Besides my mother and grandmother, he's all I have," Kelsey whispered.

"You have me now, and I won't let you go." Mythia leaned down and pressed a hard kiss to her mate's lips. Kelsey tried to speak, but Mythia didn't give her the chance. It had been hours since she'd had a taste of her mate, and that was too long. Until they completed the bond, the intensity of the mating call would grow.

Kelsey melted against Mythia as she opened her mouth. Her tongue slipped out and invited Mythia's in. Unable to resist, Mythia tilted her head to the side to deepen it, grabbing a fistful of Kelsey's thick locks.

The scent of her mate's arousal floated through the air.

A cough sounded loudly behind her.

Lifting her head, Mythia glanced over her shoulder. She had completely forgotten that Sascha and Raven were in the room.

She turned back to Kelsey to see her staring up at her with those wide, pretty eyes.

"When are the humans to arrive?" Mythia asked Sascha, keeping her eyes on her mate while running her finger along her bottom lip.

She needed her mate.

"Tomorrow evening. Once the sun settles, they will arrive," Sascha replied.

"Can I at least call him? My cell phone is in my bag."

She looked into Kelsey's eyes and knew she wouldn't be able to tell her no.

"Fine. I'll have your bag brought to you."

CHAPTER TEN

Kelsey sat on the couch and stared down at her phone. As promised, her bag was returned to her. Raven and Sascha had exited the room, leaving her alone with Mythia, who she was sure would hover close by while she placed the call to Jasper.

She tried to calm herself. Excitement filled her at the thought of hearing her friend's voice. She didn't want to appear nervous or anything, for she knew he would rush to her side.

But if what Sascha said was true, she was

sure he would be the one behind the men coming to the castle tomorrow.

"What's wrong? I thought you wanted to call this Jasper?"

"I am. I just don't know what to say."

"You tell him that you are the mate of Mythia the Black, and you are fine."

"You're known as Mythia the Black?" She had never heard of Mythia addressed as such.

"I've been known by a few names." The dragon shifter shrugged. Kelsey stared at her with the realization that she wanted to know more about the shifter.

Mate with her, a voice whispered in her head.

Kelsey jumped.

Who the hell said that? Swallowing hard, she tried to will her racing heart to slow down.

"What is it, my love?"

"Oh, nothing," Kelsey lied. Mythia didn't look convinced. Kelsey offered a small smile of assurance and turned her attention to her phone. Unlocking the screen, she tapped on Jasper's number and put the phone to her ear.

"Hello? Kelsey?" Jasper's frantic voice came on the line. Kelsey closed her eyes and inhaled slowly. She was trying not to let her emotions get the best of her. He was probably losing his mind with guilt. He had warned her about breaking into the castle.

"Jasper. It's me."

"Oh my God! Where are you? Are you safe? I'll come get you."

Out of the corner of her eye, she saw Mythia straighten to her full height. Apparently, she could hear Jasper with her shifter hearing. Her possessive dragon didn't like the mention of her leaving.

"Yes, I'm safe. I'm still at the castle."

"Just tell me where I can come pick you up. I've been going crazy. I knew I shouldn't have left you, or at least went in with you—"

"Slow down, Jasper." Kelsey tucked her hair behind her ear and rested back fully on the couch. She brought her knees up to her chest and blew out a long breath. "Look, you don't need to come and get me. I'm fine, I promise."

"What do you mean, I don't need to come and get you?"

"I'm safe. I have something to work out here."

"Did that dragon shifter hurt you? Is she keeping you hostage? Is she punishing you for breaking in?"

Kelsey's eyes met Mythia's. She wasn't sure if her friend was ready to hear how Mythia punished her.

Hurt her?

No.

Keeping her hostage?

That was debatable, since the mating bond had awoken in Mythia. She had been extremely protective and possessive. If Kelsey were to leave, or someone took her, there would be nothing to stop Mythia from coming after her. That little bit of knowledge stirred something deep inside of Kelsey.

She liked it.

"It's nothing I can't handle," she replied softly. That was the truth. The punishment was something she'd be willing to experience repeatedly.

Memories surfaced from the previous night, and she had to clench her legs together.

Her core pulsed.

"What is that supposed to mean?" he demanded.

Mythia's nose flared. She pushed off the wall and came to sit on the sofa next to Kelsey.

"It means for you not to come. I'll call you back later."

"When?"

"I don't know. But please, don't come here tomorrow." She had to try to keep him from coming here. There was no need for him and the others to storm the castle.

"How did you know about tomorrow? You know what? Don't answer. We're coming for you, Kelsey."

"Jasper, don't!"

The line went dead.

Dammit. Jasper could be so damn stubborn. He had his mind set that she needed his help. He was always her knight in shining armor when they were kids. She was always much smaller and awkward. Bullies would try to mess with her, and then he would step in and beat them up for her.

Mythia rested her hand on Kelsey's knee. "You couldn't change his mind?"

Shaking her head, Kelsey clutched her

phone tight. She didn't want things to get out of hand.

"Promise me you won't harm him or any of the people that show up. They're my friends. They just want to protect me."

"That's my job," Mythia snapped, her amber eyes glowing. Her hand tightened on Kelsey's knee.

Kelsey had to calm her dragon down and diffuse this situation. If Mythia lost her temper when the humans came, someone was bound to get hurt. She couldn't have that on your conscience. This all was her fault. She had been so set on taking back the necklace for her family.

Setting her phone down on the armrest, she turned to Mythia.

"If they attack me, then I'm obligated to respond in the same fashion."

Kelsey moved over and straddled Mythia, whose hands came to settle on her hips.

"Please." Kelsey cupped Mythia's face, her breaths coming faster. It never ceased to amaze her how her body reacted to Mythia. Her nipples pushed against the material of her bra. She groaned from the sensations that fluttered through her body. She was on edge.

Her arousal was heightened as she rubbed her breasts against Mythia's. Leaning down, she pressed a chaste kiss to Mythia's lips. "For me. I'm asking you not to hurt my friends. They care for me."

She rocked her hips against Mythia's stomach. Mythia's hands disappeared underneath her dress and skated around to her bottom, squeezing Kelsey's ample ass as she brought her flush against her.

"You care for these people?"

Kelsey kept her lips against Mythia's, nibbling on the dragon's bottom lip. Her amber eyes were locked on Kelsey's.

"I do. They're just concerned." Kelsey dragged her tongue along Mythia's lip before covering her mouth with hers. The kiss quickly grew frantic, the need to be consumed by this woman overwhelming her.

She tore her mouth away and trailed kisses along Mythia's jawline and down her neck.

"And you would do anything for them?" Mythia asked.

"Yes," she answered without hesitation. Mythia lifted her dress and pulled it over her head, leaving her in her bra and thong. The sound of her growl shot straight to Kelsey's pussy.

"It's honorable how much you want to defend them."

"I think it would be nice if you took your clothes off too." Kelsey's remark was rewarded with Mythia's laugh.

"Impatient mate." With the blink of her eyes, Mythia's clothes disappeared.

Kelsey groaned at the sight of the naked woman. Her brown skin was flawless, her breasts high and full. Her nipples were drawn into tight buds. Her stomach was flat, with a strong muscular definition.

Kelsey leaned forward and buried her face into the crook of Mythia's neck. She was going to take her time and explore dragon. It was her turn to bring pleasure to this woman.

Mythia had given her more pleasure than she ever knew existed.

She lifted Mythia's breast so she could take the nipple into her mouth. She bathed the large bud with her tongue and began suckling it. Moaning at the feel of the warm breasts in her hands, she teased Mythia with her tongue, flicking the nipple. She then moved over to the other, needing to taste them both.

Her hand cupped the other one while she took her time. Mythia's hands came to rest on the back of her head. She threaded her fingers into Kelsey's hair as if to hold her in place.

Kelsey looked up as Mythia laid her head back on the pillow. Her expression was one of pleasure. Kelsey grew elated at seeing Mythia enjoying her suckling her breasts.

She moved down off the couch to where she was able to kneel on the couch in front of Mythia and began pressing kisses to her stomach.

Mythia brought her feet to the edge of the couch and dropped her legs open for Kelsey.

Kelsey licked her lips at the sight before her.

Mythia's pussy looked perfect. No hair, fat lips, and her clit protruding out, seeking attention. It was slick and waiting for Kelsey.

"Your pussy is so pretty," Kelsey murmured, trailing her finger along Mythia's slick labia. The scent of her lover filled the air, surrounding her.

She never wanted to leave.

"Come, my love. Have your fill of my pussy." Mythia's hand slid down and spread her labia apart to explore her clit and core. Kelsey eyed the cream that was waiting for her. "It will only ever be yours from this moment forward."

She didn't have to be told twice.

She leaned down and slid her tongue along Mythia's slit before coming to stop at her clit. She captured it with her mouth and suckled it. The taste of Mythia exploded on her tongue. She moved to get closer, resting her hands on the back of Mythia's thighs.

Mythia lifted Kelsey's hair out of the way while encouraging her on.

Kelsey tugged on her clit before soothing it with her tongue. She slid her tongue back down, gathering Mythia's cream. Mythia's body shook from her sensual assault.

Kelsey pushed two fingers inside of her and gently began to fuck her with them while concentrating on her swollen nub. Her moans were driving Kelsey insane.

She had always loved eating pussy, and was a pro at it. But none of the other women mattered. The only one she wanted to ensure she brought pleasure to was Mythia.

She pumped her fingers in and out while continuing to suck on her clit.

Mythia's grip on her hair tightened, and she welcomed the pain.

"Tell me you love the taste of my pussy," Mythia demanded, rocking her hips forward, trying to ride Kelsey's face. "I can scent the wetness between your thighs."

The juices were practically running down Kelsey's legs. She had never been so turned on before.

"I love the taste of you," Kelsey admitted. Their eyes met for a second, and something passed between them. Kelsey felt it in her chest as her fingers continued to pump. She twirled them around so she could search for Mythia's G-spot.

Dropping her head, she took Mythia's clit back into her mouth, loving how Mythia writhed at her touch. The sexy whimpers coming from the strong dragon shifter were fueling the fire she felt for Mythia.

"Goddess above," Mythia grunted before pulling Kelsey's head back. Lifting Kelsey easily from the floor, Mythia had her laid out on the couch in one swift move.

Her bra and thong met a disastrous end as Mythia ripped them from her body like tearing a piece of paper. She tugged the shards of material and tossed them over her shoulder.

"I did like those, you know," Kelsey protested. She was a sucker for sexy lingerie and owned plenty.

"I'll buy you as much as you want." Mythia's amber eyes bored into Kelsey's. She leaned down and pressed a hard kiss to Kelsey's lips. "There is nothing I can't afford."

"Promises, promises." She was getting a kick out of Mythia's reactions.

"I'll prove it." Mythia swooped down and covered Kelsey's mouth with hers, the kiss hard and controlling. Mythia controlled every little bit of it with her tongue darting in and stroking Kelsey's.

Kelsey gasped when Mythia broke the kiss. Her body was on fire, and the only person capable of putting her out of her misery was Mythia.

Sitting back, she spread Kelsey's legs

wide. Her hand slipped between her thighs and her confident finger parted her labia. She trailed her finger through the proof of her arousal and brought some of the wetness up to Kelsey's clit.

"You're always so wet for me, my love."

Kelsey was unable to respond. Her hips rocked to meet Mythia's fingers as they rubbed her sensitive bundle of nerves. Ripples of desire were washing through Kelsey. She released a frustrated groan when Mythia paused her hand.

The dragon shifter had the nerve to grin.

"You want your release, don't you?"

Kelsey's panic began to surface. Mythia wasn't going to hold her orgasm hostage, was she? At the moment, Kelsey was prepared to beg for release.

"Yes, please," she whispered, pushing her hips forward to meet Mythia's nimble fingers. The motion sent a jolt of lightning through her body as her clit brushed Mythia's hand.

"Tonight, I won't deny you anything. I'll give you so much, you'll beg me to stop," Mythia promised.

Kelsey truly doubted she would.

She was addicted to everything about the dragon shifter.

Widening her legs, Mythia positioned herself over Kelsey. Her heart skipped a beat at the sight of Mythia lowering her wet pussy atop of hers.

They both groaned aloud once their cunts connected. Kelsey's arousal was growing higher. There was nothing more intimate than the position they were in.

She whimpered, trying to hold still. Her eyes were locked on the full breasts near her face. Those brown nipples were calling to her.

Mythia's hand skated along her stomach, breasts, and came to rest on the column of her neck. Her thumb brushed the side of Kelsey's neck, and she had a vision of Mythia sinking her fangs into that exact spot.

"Mine." Mythia's growl was low, possessive, and sexy as hell. She tightened her grip ever so slightly and began to rock her hips. Kelsey reached her hands over her head and gripped the sofa cushion. She had a feeling this was going to be one hell of a ride.

She gasped at the sensation of their slick nubs brushing against each other. It felt so good that she turned all of her pleasure over to Mythia. She could trust that this woman would see to her.

Kelsey raised her hips to meet Mythia's. She took in her expression and found nothing but pure pleasure etched on her face. Mythia's eyes were closed, and she began to increase the pace of their rhythmic movements.

Their moans fluttered through the air. Her body was burning up with a fine sheen of sweat coating her. They continued to thrust and rub each other. The nerve endings in her body were frazzled. There was so much pleasure coursing through her body at the moment, she knew she wasn't going to last much longer.

Kelsey cried out, thrusting harder. The grip along her neck tightened even more, and she loved the feeling of the possessive hold.

It was a statement.

She belonged to Mythia.

There was no argument, for she knew it to be true. Kelsey closed her eyes and fell into the moment. With the feel of their combined juices coating their inner thighs, she was finding it hard to hold herself still.

"More," she whimpered.

"Yes, mate. I'll give you more," Mythia asserted. Their movements became frenzied as they both sought their release. Hard and fast, Mythia thrust her hips in hot, circular motions. Her hand tightening to where it left Kelsey taking short gasps of air. She was floating along the clouds of her euphoric journey.

Kelsey couldn't hold back any longer. Her orgasm burst forth, sending waves of ecstasy through her body. She screamed as her body arched off the couch.

Mythia maintained a tight hold on her while her grunts turned into cries of ecstasy as she too reached her climax. A warmth bathed Kelsey's center as Mythia's release escaped her.

A strong burst of energy surged through the air.

Mythia collapsed on top of Kelsey while they both panted, trying to catch their breath. Wrapping her arms around Mythia, Kelsey held her in place.

This was her mate.

Her dragon shifter.

She would never let her go.

Maybe the need to reclaim her family's heirloom was fate sending her to her destiny.

They lay together until they were both breathing at a normal rate. Kelsey didn't care to know how much time had passed. This moment was precious to her.

Something had shifted between them.

She had fallen for the dragon shifter.

Mythia lifted her head up and met her gaze. Kelsey reached for her face and brought her down for a kiss.

No words were needed.

CHAPTER ELEVEN

Mythia walked into the bedroom and found Kelsey standing by the window in their bedroom.

Mythia didn't require much sleep. Her dragon was barely able to settle knowing that Xomor was going to try and figure out who his kin was that had touched the medallion.

She had left the room to allow Kelsey to rest. Their lovemaking in the sunroom had only been the beginning. She'd brought her mate to their bedroom, where it had continued on for hours. Her dragon was insatiable when it came to their mate.

She was pleased that Kelsey appeared to keep pace with her.

After multiple orgasms, her little human finally fell into a hard slumber.

The desire for her mate remained strong. Instead of waking Kelsey again so she could have her, Mythia left the room. She'd went down to the library and tried to research the connection that Xomor claimed he had on the Rose family.

She'd kept centuries of records, but couldn't find what she was looking for. She sent an urgent message to Galdar, her older brother. She hadn't spoked to the grumpy dragon in at least fifty years. His lair was located in the Rif Mountains along the Mediterranean coastline of Morocco, and it was rare for him to venture into her part of the world.

If anyone could trace down a family lineage, her brother could. She just had to wait for him to contact her. Afterward, she had gone to speak with Fiona to request a special breakfast for them.

She quietly made her way across the room while taking Kelsey in. She was dressed in a white floor length silk robe, and her dark hair was left to fall freely around her shoulders. Mythia arrived behind Kelsey and slid her arms around her waist, pulling her back to her.

She nuzzled her face into the crook of Kelsey's neck. "Morning, mate."

"I wondered where you went," Kelsey murmured, a hint of a smile in her voice as she rested back into Mythia's embrace. Satisfaction swelled inside Mythia's chest. Her mate was accepting her.

"Was my mate missing me?" Mythia inhaled the light floral scent lingering on her mate's neck.

"I was. I don't think I like waking up without you next to me," Kelsey admitted softly. She pulled her hair to the opposite side of her neck as if to offer it to Mythia.

"Just know that if I do have to leave before you wake, I will always return to you." Mythia's tongue glided along her soft skin as her hand traveled up Kelsey's stomach to her breasts.

Mythia growled. The mating bond was calling to her, demanding she claim her mate.

Not yet.

She hadn't even revealed the hoard she

had collected for Kelsey. Tonight, she would do so.

Dragon claiming tradition called for her to present the many treasures she had collected to her mate. If her mate was pleased and accepted, then she would claim her.

She grew slightly nervous.

What if everything she had wasn't enough?

There had been a few rejections in the history of dragon claiming. Those dragons who were rejected by their mates had gone insane.

Mythia inhaled sharply. The fates wouldn't do that to her. Kelsey was hers. If she wasn't happy with the amount of treasure waiting for her, Mythia would scour the earth's surface for even more gold, silver, and diamonds, until Kelsey would have no other choice but to accept her.

"You promise?" Kelsey's quiet question rivaled something in Mythia.

Her gums burned and stretched as her sharp fangs burst forth. She scraped them along Kelsey's skin, making her tremble.

"Always," Mythia growled. This was one promise she would keep. The urge to pierce

Kelsey's neck was growing, but she would have to resist.

She brushed open the robe, exposing her beautiful mate's body. The sun's rays highlighted her tanned skin and rosy nipples. Mythia took her breast in her hand again, pinching Kelsey's budded nipple. Her mate cried out and leaned her head back onto Mythia's shoulder.

Mythia's other hand lowered to Kelsey's soft belly to her plump, parted lips, finding her mate's pussy coated in her arousal. Groaning, Mythia slid her finger through the wetness, then rubbed it over Kelsey's clit.

"Mine." She nipped at her skin, but not enough to break it. She began rubbing small circles on Kelsey's swollen bud.

"Yes, I'm yours," Kelsey breathed. Her body arched off Mythia's as she writhed in her arms.

Mythia increased her pace while applying more pressure to her bundle of nerves. She pinched and pulled on Kelsey's nipple, making her moan.

"Take your pleasure, my love."

Kelsey threw her head back and screamed. The tremors shook through her body so hard, Mythia had to tighten her hold to keep her from falling.

Finally, Kelsey fell back against Mythia, panting heavily. Mythia continued to rub in slow, rhythmic motions as she came down, enjoying the feel of Kelsey's warm release.

Kelsey turned her face toward Mythia, seeking her lips. Mythia rewarded her with a deep, passionate kiss as she pulled her hand out from between Kelsey's thighs.

Mythia spun them around and backed Kelsey up until the back of her legs hit the bed. She tore her lips from Kelsey's and brought her fingers to her lips. Kelsey grew still, watching her lick each of her fingers clean of her release.

"You're so fucking tasty," Mythia chuckled, running her tongue along her middle finger, lapping up the last bit of cream.

Bending down, she lifted Kelsey up by the back of her thighs and laid her out on the bed. Spreading Kelsey's legs wide, she covered her pussy with her mouth.

Kelsey rested her head against the crook of Mythia's arm, their warm, naked bodies entwined together. Her breasts were pressed against Mythia's, but she scooted even closer, not wanting any space between them.

Mythia's fingers slowly trailed along Kelsey's back. Even though it was soft, soothing sensations, it was also arousing.

How could she possibly be ready to again?

Kelsey closed her eyes and sighed, basking in the feeling of Mythia tightening her hold around her.

She felt safe, protected, and loved.

She didn't know what she needed to be protected from, but she knew Mythia would defend her against anything.

Her thoughts drifted to the medallion on the nightstand. They hadn't spoken about the weird thing that had occurred when she'd touched it.

"What was that when I touched the necklace?" she asked. It had been frightening to think that her touching it caused something bad to happen.

"The ruby medallion had a curse on it," Mythia began. Kelsey stiffened at the announcement. She had never heard of it being cursed.

"Cursed? By who?"

"That's what I need to find out." Kelsey looked up and found Mythia staring at the ceiling. "But I know why the curse was placed on it."

Kelsey sensed this conversation was about to go deep. Pushing up from her position, she leaned back against the pillows while Mythia rolled over to her back, forcing the sheets lower, revealing her brown breasts.

Kelsey tried to keep from staring at them. They were perfect in every way. Memories of her mouth on them came to mind—

She cleared her throat and tore her eyes away from the brown mounds and to Mythia's face. "Why was it cursed?"

"What do you know about your family's line?"

"Nothing more than what my mother and grandmother have shared with me. As for my father's side, I don't know anything about him, nor have I ever met him."

They sat in a comfortable silence for what seemed like minutes, but was only seconds. Kelsey wasn't sure where Mythia was going with her line of questioning.

Mythia pushed up on her elbow and announced, "I believe you have dragon blood in you."

"There's always been a joke about me being one sixteenth on my mother's father's side." Her mother had shared that with her when she was younger.

"This is not a joke, and I believe you're more than what you think. If you don't know your father and his lineage, it could be possible that there's a dragon kin on his side too." Mythia sat up and took Kelsey's hand in hers. The seriousness in her expression worried Kelsey.

"What are you saying?"

"This explains how you're able to sense the mating bond, your easy acceptance of fate, your comfortable nature around me."

"Are you saying I can shift into a dragon?"

"No." A small smile played on Mythia's lips. "What I'm saying is, because of the blood running through your veins, you are special."

She pressed a kiss to Kelsey's fingers.

Kelsey moved closer to her, but Mythia held her back.

"Remember when you mentioned the man from your time walk journey?"

"The one you fought."

"He has claimed that the curse was placed on the medallion. He is bound to it."

"What?" she exclaimed. Her heart began to race. Was he going to do her harm for touching the necklace? "Why would he be bound to my family's necklace?"

"Because he is your ancestor. Any one of his kin who owns and touches it he will come to protect you."

Kelsey paused at the thought that not only was it just confirmed she had dragon kin in her lineage, but that he was still around. He wanted to protect her? Did that mean get to know her and her family? Walk amongst them?

"That doesn't sound too bad. If I'm his kin, and he wants to be—"

"He will take you from me," Mythia growled, her grip tightening on Kelsey. "Per dragon law, an unmated member of a dragon's family, no matter how many times removed, will be placed under that dragon's protection."

"But I don't want to leave."

"I'm in the middle of trying to confirm his claim. I'm waiting for my brother to get back with me." Mythia gathered her into her arms, and Kelsey leaned into her warm embrace. "He is the keeper of all dragon lineages. He'll know if Xomor's claim is true."

She didn't want to be taken from Mythia.

That scary looking man was her ancestor? She shuddered at the memory of his angry eyes.

"And if it is, how do we stop it?" Kelsey pulled back and met Mythia's amber gaze.

"You must be claimed by your mate. Then, his claim will be voided."

"Then do it." The words escaped her lips before she even had a chance to think. It was an automatic response, because she knew it was what was meant to be.

She belonged to Mythia.

Kelsey moved on the bed and straddled Mythia's lap, presenting her neck to her.

"Make me yours," she breathed. Her core clenched at the thought of Mythia sinking her sharp fangs into her flesh. Everything

Mythia shared with her about dragon's blood made complete sense to her. If she had dragon on her father's side, that would enhance her connection with them.

What would make even more sense was for Mythia to put her mark on her now.

Mythia took hold of Kelsey's chin and tipped her face down to meet her gaze.

"It's not that easy."

"Why not? Don't you just bite me and the magic happens?" She wrapped her arms around Mythia's neck, bringing her face between her breasts. She wasn't above using sexual favors to get what she wanted from her woman.

Mythia inhaled and rubbed her face along Kelsey's sternum while cupping Kelsey's ass.

"There's this thing called tradition." Mythia's response was muffled. Her tongue slid along Kelsey's chest before she lifted her face. "There's something we need to do."

"And what might that be?" Kelsey rotated her hips around, grinding down on Mythia's lap. She'd had a healthy sexual appetite before, but now it was mind-boggling how much she needed sex.

And not just with anyone.

Mythia.

"Not that," Mythia murmured. "Though they do go together quite well.

"Whatever we have to do, I want to do it." Kelsey was starting to breathe heavier, growing more aroused as the seconds ticked by.

"Then we shall. But first, I must take care of you."

Kelsey jerked as something appeared on Mythia's body. She looked down and found Mythia fitted with a monster sized strap-on. The cock was long with a thick girth. Her hand automatically dropped to it. She couldn't wrap her small hand around it.

"This is too big," Kelsey chuckled nervously as she eyed it. She'd never taken one that big before. It looked like it could split her in two.

"You're going to take it, my love. Do you trust me?" Mythia raised her perfectly sculpted brow. The commanding tone in Mythia's voice didn't go over her head.

Her woman was telling her she didn't have a choice.

Kelsey moaned, loving how her dragon

mate knew just what she needed and provided it.

She leaned forward and pressed her lips to Mythia's. This time, she controlled the kiss.

Mythia helped lift her up, the tip of the hard shaft nudging the entrance of her soaked pussy. She lowered herself down, taking the first inch. She paused, breathing harder, then closed her eyes, focusing on the sensation of being stretched.

Mythia pushed up slightly, introducing more of it into her.

"Oh, God," she panted as she continued to slide down. She didn't stop until it was buried fully inside of her. She couldn't believe she was able to take something so big.

Kelsey rocked her hips slowly, testing herself out. There was no pain, only pleasure. She lifted herself up and glided slowly down again, her body accommodating it with ease.

A shudder rippled through her.

"Have all the fun you want, mate," Mythia asserted, her amber eyes blazing with desire. She captured Kelsey's breast with her teeth, biting down on it, sending a jolt all through Kelsey's body.

Her body moved on autopilot. The pleasure coursing through her as the cock slid in and out of her was overwhelming. Mythia began to pump her hips, sending it unbelievably deeper. She cried out, her movements becoming more frenzied as she raced after her release.

"Yes," she hissed, bouncing up and down. Mythia rolled them over until she was on her back, the cock still lodged deep inside her.

Mythia took over.

Hard and fast, she took Kelsey, keeping a steady pace that had her on the edge, ready to come.

Adjusting their position, Mythia pushed her legs back and rested her hands on the back of her thighs. It allowed her to sink so deep, Kelsey saw stars.

She gasped, no longer able to hold back.

Her body detonated. The pleasure exploded within her, taking her breath away. She rode the waves of the most intense orgasm she'd ever experience.

Mythia continued to thrust, not giving her any relief. The cock slid into effortlessly, hitting every corner of her channel. The ecstasy from it moving inside of her was life-altering.

"Mythia!" she screamed as another wave of pleasure crashed into her, sending her into another soul-searing orgasm. It was so intense, tears spilled uncontrollably down her cheeks.

Mythia thrust one last time, lodging deep inside of her. She'd never felt so full before in her life. There was nothing like it.

She held onto Mythia with what little strength she had.

If she were to die from pleasure today, she would go out one happy woman.

CHAPTER TWELVE

Kelsey gasped. "This is beautiful." She glanced down at the dress Mythia had conjured. It was misty rose and fit her perfectly, hugging every curve. The neckline plunged to her waist, as did the back. The material was sheer, revealing the outline of her areolas. Her dark hair flowed down her back, tickling her skin.

Mythia waved her hand, and a white rose appeared behind her ear, keeping her hair tucked off to the side, leaving her neck exposed.

"You are beautiful," Mythia murmured.

She was dressed in her leather pants and boots, with a matching leather cuirass with her family emblem embossed on it. Her hair was plaited into an intricate detail.

"This magic of yours saves so much time getting dressed," Kelsey joked, smiling.

Mythia's beast was pleased that their mate appeared to be happy with them so far. She swallowed hard, knowing the trust test would be in a few minutes. Since her mate was too impatient to wait until nightfall for the traditional presentation, they would do it now.

She hadn't heard from her brother yet, but that didn't mean anything. Deep inside, she knew that Xomor spoke the truth. There was no reason for him to lie. He appeared seconds after Kelsey touched the medallion.

She walked over to Kelsey, unable to resist her beauty. "Are you ready?"

Kelsey held up her hand. "You stay over there."

"What?" Mythia paused, confused. Had she done something to offend her mate?

"Every time you're near me, I get all horny, and then we end up there." She pointed to the bed.

"It's the natural process of mating, my love. We will always yearn for each other," she explained.

"Always?" Kelsey's eyes widened. She ran her hands along her waist and played with the skirts. "I can't even look at you without feeling myself growing wet and soaking my panties. Then there's an ache here when you aren't near me." She rested her hand on her chest, over her heart.

Mythia closed the gap between them.

"It's the mating bond," she whispered. She was secretly pleased that her mate was affected. It just proved what she had known since the moment they had met. "But don't worry, mate. I will always take care of your pleasure. I told you it belonged to me."

"Yes," Kelsey breathed, pressing closer to Mythia. Her eyes were dilated, and the pulse at the base of her neck was racing. Mythia reached up and trailed her fingers along Kelsey's temple, down to her chin.

Mythia inhaled the faint scent of Kelsey's arousal.

Her hand continued its trek. She traced Kelsey's lips, still swollen from her kisses, down to her throat, and then to her chest.

She brushed her thumb over Kelsey's areola, teasing her. Kelsey's nipples grew into taut buds, pushing against the material of the dress.

Mythia had to stop this before they did end up back in bed.

She wrapped her arm around Kelsey so she could teleport them to the vault. "Come."

"Don't you ever just walk through the castle?"

Mythia shrugged. "Once in a while."

"Will you give me the official tour?"

"But of course." Tightening her hold on Kelsey, she focused on where she wanted to go. They immediately vanished from the bedroom and arrived outside the vault within seconds.

"Hey," Kelsey laughed as she stepped away from Mythia, taking a look at her surroundings. "I thought you were going to give me a tour?"

"We can do that later. The castle has been here for hundreds of years. It's not going anywhere." Mythia took her hand and walked to the large steel door.

"You know, I thought the medallion would be in here," Kelsey admitted. She moved to stand before Mythia and rested her hands on it. Turning around, she leaned her back against it. "I assumed that since the castle was so old, the vault would be something I could jimmy a lock and break into."

"Is that so?" Mythia moved in front of Kelsey, trapping her against the door. She leaned down and pressed a soft kiss to her lips. "You just assumed that I never updated anything here?"

"How was I supposed to know? Now that I think of it, for someone worth billions, you should have the latest technology."

"And how do you know how much I'm worth? Were you researching me?" Mythia kissed her again.

"For someone who has lived a long life such as you, I'd be worried if you weren't worth a lot of money."

Mythia barked out a hefty laugh. She would have to agree. She didn't think she knew any dragon shifters who were poor.

She dragged herself away from Kelsey and moved over to the panel on the wall. Entering her numeric password, she then placed her fingertips on the scanner. The locking mechanisms sounded as the vault opened.

Kelsey jumped away from it and came to stand my Mythia.

She took her mate's hand in hers, pride filling her chest. She had worked so hard for so long, and now the final moment was upon her.

The door opened halfway and then stopped. There was enough room for them to walk through. Mythia guided Kelsey behind her. The floodlights turned on as they moved past the initial opening.

"Oh, my." Kelsey released Mythia's hand and walked ahead of her. The room was filled with countless rows of shelving. Mythia had tried to remain as organized as she could. She never was one to just pile everything up to the ceiling. She had wanted her mate to be able to locate and find whatever treasure she wanted or needed.

Mythia tried to see the room through Kelsey's eyes.

Her mate ambled over to a table that held many baskets on it, each one holding some-thing interesting.

She trailed behind Kelsey, her heart pounding a mile a minute. She had faced down the deadliest of foes in hand-to-hand combat, fought vicious dragons, vampires, and other shifters in her lifetime, yet nothing came close to the amount of fear that was mounting inside of her.

What if this wasn't enough?

"This is beautiful." Kelsey reached into a basket and pulled out a jeweled hair-clip encrusted with diamonds and emeralds. The diamonds sparkled in the light. Replacing it, she backed away from the table and turned around in a circle, taking in the entire room.

Her gaze landed on Kelsey.

"You collected all of this?"

She jerked her head in a nod since her tongue was stuck to the roof of her mouth. Kelsey spun back around and kept walking. Her feet sped up as she went to another table, then over to a shelving unit. Her face lit up at countless items that she touched. Mythia continued to trail behind her, enjoying Kelsey's reactions.

Kelsey came to the canvas that depicted two naked women lying on a plush chaise. It was Mythia's favorite piece. She didn't say a word as she stared at it. Minutes passed before she turned to Mythia.

Mythia panicked at the sight of tears

trailing down her face.

"What is all of this?" she asked, spreading her arms wide. Sniffing, she wiped her face with the back of her hand.

"This is the collection of treasures I've amassed over my lifetime. Dragons scour the world in search of the perfect gifts and trinkets for their mates."

She came to stand in front of Kelsey and knelt down on one knee.

This was a very vulnerable position for a dragon to be in.

"For their mates?"

"Yes. I have been preparing my entire life for this moment. We are destined to be together. I vow to always protect you, provide for you, and pleasure you." Mythia searched Kelsey's face, and didn't see anything but awe and wonder, so she continued on. "I will never love another person. You are for me, Kelsey. Please say you accept my treasure, my dragon, and me."

Kelsey didn't say anything. She tore her gaze away from Mythia and looked around the room. Mythia's heart pounded as she waited.

"Oh, Mythia. The only thing I truly need

is you and your dragon," Kelsey said. Mythia jumped to her feet and pulled Kelsey to her. Lowering her head, she took her in a long, passionate kiss.

She teleported them to the little nook in the corner that was decorated with thick rugs and oversized pillows. It was her little oasis. A place she would come to relax and be around her treasure. Mythia glanced at the scones on the walls and blew a puff of air toward them. Fire flared to life, lighting the candles. Mythia lowered the lights to the vault, basking the room in darkness. The candlelight was all she would need.

"What is this area?"

Mythia guided her into the midst of the pillows. "I come here when I want to relax and dream," she admitted. Taking Kelsey's hand in hers, she pressed a kiss to the back of it. "Get down on your knees."

Kelsey's eyes widened, but without a word, she did as she was told.

"After today, your life will be forever changed. Accepting me as your mate will mean that you will walk throughout time by my side. You will no longer age. You will live longer than your family. "

"But I'll have you."

Mythia's heart softened.

"You will always have me." Mythia turned her attention to the box resting on the shelf along the wall. She had prepared this area in the hopes that she would one day claim her mate here. She took it down and placed it on the floor beside her.

Mythia moved closer to Kelsey and knelt down in front of her, putting them at eye level with each other. Her gums stretched and burned as her fangs descended. The air grew electric. The fates were looking down on them with their blessing.

Mythia's magic was maintained. As much as her dragon wanted to break free to meet Kelsey, she knew she would have to wait. Soon they would, and she'd even take Kelsey out for a flight.

Mythia trailed her fingers down the side of Kelsey's neck, brushing away the runaway strands of her hair, and held it at an angle.

Leaning forward, Mythia ran her tongue along the same path. The pulse at the base of Kelsey's neck spiked.

The candlelight flickered.

The tension in the air thickened.

She gathered Kelsey close and sunk her fangs into her mate's shoulder. Kelsey's body arched toward her, even as she whimpered. Mythia's dragon roared, spewing fire to celebrate the claiming of their mate.

Mythia lifted her head. Kelsey's eyes were shut, and her breaths were coming fast. Mythia lowered her onto the pillows and laid with her mate while the enzymes from her bite coursed through her body.

She wouldn't change into a dragon, but the chemistry of her body would be altered. Kelsey would cease to age. She would live a long life with Mythia. Dragons could live for thousands of years.

Mythia hadn't even reached her prime yet.

She licked Kelsey's wound to slow the bleeding until it stopped.

Mythia trailed her fingers along Kelsey's face, waiting for her body to relax. She had never taken a mate before, but from what she was told, it could take some time for humans to acclimate to their new genetic makeup.

"Are you okay, my love?" Mythia asked softly.

Kelsey's eyes fluttered open. She turned

her head and met Mythia's gaze, smiling.

"That was something." Capturing Mythia's hand, she pressed a kiss to it. "At first, there was slight pain from the bite, but then it immediately went away. I can't describe it. I felt as if I were high, floating with the clouds."

Mythia nodded, entwining their fingers together.

"There is one more step, my love. We need to completely seal the bond now while the enzymes are still working through you." Her mate would be weak for just a little longer before the strength of Mythia's dragon energized her.

Mythia sat forward and grabbed the box that was on the floor. She opened it and removed a small silver dagger with a pearl handle. It was handed down to her by her mother, and had been in her family for centuries.

Kelsey's eyes followed her movements.

"I will cut my finger, and you will drink the blood. This will seal the bond."

"The bite of a dragon, the blood of the dragon..." Kelsey murmured as she reached out to place her hand on Mythia's heart.

"And the heart of a dragon. Forever will I be yours."

Mythia paused and stared at Kelsey.

"How do you know that?" It was the ancient vow dragons were to say to their mate at the completion of the claiming ritual.

Kelsey looked up at the ceiling and frowned. "I don't know. It just came to me."

Mythia nicked her finger with the dagger and sat it down as Kelsey turned to her and opened her mouth. Mythia slipped her finger inside to allow Kelsey to drink from her open wound. Kelsey's hand came up and held onto her wrist.

Her mate held her gaze while she sucked Mythia's finger.

"Now I am to say those words to you, mate," Mythia chuckled. She was going to have to concentrate hard, because the sensation of Kelsey sucking the blood from her finger was turning quite erotic. "Kelsey Rose. The bite of a dragon, the blood of the dragon, and the heart of my dragon. Forever, I will be yours."

"And I yours," Kelsey replied, releasing Mythia's hand. Her body arched off the pillows as a cry tore from her lips. Her flower fell from her hair and disappeared in between the pillows.

Within minutes, the change was done.

Their bond was sealed.

The dragon was officially bonded to her thief.

"Mythia," Kelsey moaned, a blush creeping up her neck and spreading across her cheeks.

Mythia inhaled, taking in the aroma of her mate's arousal.

"Will this intense need to be with you ever go away?" Kelsey questioned.

Mythia waved her hand over Kelsey's body and the dress disappeared, leaving her naked. She got rid of her clothing as well. Now that they were officially mated, the need to have each other would increase.

"It will never go away, my love." Mythia rolled herself on top of Kelsey and settled into the valley of her legs. Kelsey groaned and wrapped her arms around Mythia's neck. She began kissing Mythia's neck while rotating her hips. Mythia took hold of her chin and forced her to look her in the eyes. "I took a vow to pleasure you. Now let me keep my promise."

CHAPTER THIRTEEN

Kelsey stood on the stairs of the castle and waited next to Mythia, who was staring off into the distance.

"Maybe they aren't coming," Kelsey said to break the silence. Her nerves were getting the best of her. According to Sascha, Jasper and the others were coming to try to take her back. She had made Mythia promise she wouldn't hurt anyone.

"They are near." Mythia closed her eyes and went still. Kelsey wasn't sure what she was doing.

Sascha stood on the other side of Mythia.

The older woman had immediately congratulated them when she saw the mark on Kelsey's shoulder.

Kelsey was still in shock about the amount of treasure Mythia had collected over her entire life. The woman had knelt down before her and offered everything she ever had in hopes that she would accept her.

Kelsey had witnessed the slight fear in Mythia's eyes as she waited for Kelsey to answer. It was the most vulnerable she had ever seen Mythia. If she hadn't already realized she had fallen in love with her, she definitely would have fallen in love with her at that moment.

After they had consummated their mating, Mythia had conjured a new outfit for her that wasn't as revealing. The dress's bodice was fitted and low-cut, but the skirt flowed out and billowed around her ankles.

Mythia opened her eyes and looked up at the sky as she made her way down the stairs.

The hairs on Kelsey's arms stood on end. She glanced over at Sascha, who was also staring up at the sky.

The sun going down and would be setting soon.

"What is it?" Kelsey asked. There was something coming. She could feel it too. She didn't know what, but trouble was on the horizon.

The sounds of vehicles making their way along the road reached her. Kelsey stood frozen, praying Jasper and the guys weren't going to do something stupid. She stared off toward the wooded road and caught sight of headlights.

There were a few trucks headed their way. Mythia turned and focused her attention on the trucks as they came into view.

"We must get the humans out of here soon," Sascha muttered.

Kelsey's head snapped toward the seer in shock. What did she just say?

"Why?"

The seer stood with her hands facing the sky, appearing to be in some sort of trance. Were the gods sharing something with her?

A chill skated down Kelsey's spine.

"He's coming," Sascha murmured.

"You're going to have to have your friends leave immediately." Mythia leveled Kelsey with her intense gaze, her amber eyes glowing brightly.

"Okay. I'll send them away." She took the stairs and came to stand by Mythia. Whatever was headed their way, Mythia would take care of it. Kelsey was going to trust her mate and not ask questions.

The vehicles flew toward them and drew to a halt a few hundred feet away. Kelsey's eyes met Jasper's. She automatically stepped in front of Mythia as the men began exiting their vehicles.

"Kelsey," Jasper called out.

She took in all the guys: Kevin, Harvey, Don, Alfie, and James, with a few others she didn't recognize.

What had her heart leaping in her throat were the guns in their hands.

"Um, Jasper?" She moved to step forward, but Mythia's hand shot out and took hold of her arm.

"Don't go near them," Mythia snapped.

"Let her go!" Jasper shouted. Lifting his rifle, he pointed it at Mythia.

"Don't!" Kelsey shouted back with her arms raised, stepping back in front of Mythia. She didn't want to chance her mate getting shot.

"You do not protect me, mate," Mythia

growled, her hands resting on Kelsey's shoulders. She tried to move Kelsey out of the way, but she resisted.

"Jasper, I need you and the fellas to go home," Kelsey called out.

"Fuck no! I'm not leaving without you!"

"I told you that I was fine." He just had to be so damn stubborn.

Mythia wrapped an arm around her waist, lifted her, and sat her down on the ground behind her.

"She has told you twice to leave. She has been nice. If I have to tell you, I won't be."

"You can't keep her hostage!" Kevin snapped. Kelsey leaned her forehead against Mythia's back, praying there wasn't a gun in his hand. It didn't sound as if he had been drinking, but it was Kevin. He was a functioning drunk. Most times, people wouldn't even know he was wasted.

"Who's a hostage?" Mythia pulled Kelsey to her side and kept her arm around her. "Kelsey is far from a hostage. Ask her if she wants to leave."

"He's going to be here soon. These humans need to go," Sascha warned.

Kelsey's heart raced. Was she talking

about Xomor? That brought fear to Kelsey. She didn't want Mythia to go off and fight him. She had just gotten her mate, and she didn't want to chance losing her.

"Who's coming?" The guys grew nervous. They eyed the sky as if sensing what Sascha and Mythia did.

"Jasper, I love you very much." Kelsey took a step forward, but the sound of Mythia's low growl behind her kept her from going any farther. "If our friendship means anything to you, you have to trust me and leave. Now. I promise I'll explain everything soon." Tears blurred her vision. She didn't want anyone to get hurt on her account. Guns and a jealous dragon would not fare well.

"Just tell me why you can't leave right now." He turned his attention to Mythia. "If she's not a hostage, let her go."

"Never," Mythia hissed, brandishing her fangs.

"Then we'll take her back. We're not afraid of you." The guns were raised and pointed at Mythia. Kelsey flew in front of her and threw her hands up. Mythia's growl was growing louder. She didn't know how much longer she would be able to keep her mate from going after her friends, and pointing guns in her face wasn't helping.

Kelsey had to diffuse the situation fast.

"I don't want to go!" Kelsey shouted angrily. "She's right, I'm not her prisoner. I'm her mate."

The roar of a dragon shook the ground around them. Kelsey stumbled, trying to keep from falling to the ground. Mythia's steady hand held her up.

"You must go inside now," Mythia commanded before facing the direction the sound had come from.

Kelsey looked up and saw a large blue dragon fly overhead. It was a magnificent looking animal. She had never seen one like it before. Her feet were rooted in the same spot as she took in the beautiful beast before it disappeared from sight.

Yelling and slamming car doors interrupted her thoughts.

"Kelsey!" Jasper was racing toward her.

"No! Go back. Get in the truck!" she hollered as she rushed to meet him, ignoring Mythia calling her name.

They met in the middle. He tried to grab

her hand and pull her with him, but she pulled away.

"I said I'm staying."

"Did she put a spell on you?" he asked.

"No. She's my mate." She pulled the neckline of her dress away so he could see Mythia's mark. "You know what this means."

"I don't want to lose you," he admitted sadly.

"You won't, I promise. When everything is settled, we'll have a long talk so I can explain everything." Reaching up to cup his cheeks, he stilled and stared into her eyes. Whatever he saw there must have been enough for him. "You're family. We won't be apart from each other, I swear."

She didn't want to think that one day he would pass away from old age while she would remain the same age for thousands of years. She made a vow to herself that she would cherish their friendship forever.

The ground shook again with the roar of the angry dragon.

"Kelsey!" Mythia shouted again.

"Go," Kelsey whispered. Wrapping her arms around him in a quick hug, he dropped a kiss on top of her head before releasing her.

As he backed away, his eyes locked on hers as the group was scrambling and returning to their trucks.

She offered him a smile before she turned and jogged toward Mythia and Sascha, who were standing at the base of the front steps.

The sky darkened again. This time, the shadow was larger than before. She heard her name screamed again. She lifted her gaze to the sky, but she was too late. Her body was jerked up into the air.

Large talons encircled her waist and held on tight.

Kelsey screamed. The ground was growing distant, and fast. The dragon carrying her off was moving as fast as the wind.

Panic flooded her. She tried to find something she could hold on to. What if he just decided to drop her? She would never survive.

Her eyes moved back to the ground below, and she screamed. Even the tall trees appeared small. The castle was growing smaller off in the distance.

"Mythia!" she cried out.

* * *

Mythia took off running in the direction Xomor flew away in. He was carrying her mate off into the sky. Mythia picked up her speed as she got closer to the cliff. She dove off the edge of the mountain, the air whipping through her hair. She gave into her animal as she fell.

The magic of her beast took over. She shifted within seconds into her oversized black dragon.

Her wings straightened her out and began to lift her higher.

Mythia's gaze zeroed in on the blue dragon. If he harmed Kelsey in any way, she would kill him.

She pushed her animal to fly faster. Xomor may have a short head start on her, but she would catch up to him. He had the most precious thing in the world in the grasp of his talons.

She roared her frustration. There would be no mid-air fight since he had Kelsey. She followed close behind, not wanting to piss him off and risk him dropping Kelsey.

He had said that he was her ancestor and

was bound to protect her, but she would never trust him.

He now had no claim on Kelsey.

They had completed the mating bond, and that would void any hold he would've had over Kelsey.

Mythia cursed her brother. He had yet to connect with her. Galdar would catch an earful once she got hold of him.

Once Kelsey was back home, safe, Mythia had half a mind to fly to her brother and see him in person. This wasn't like him to not answer.

Xomor headed toward a secluded hillside. Dipping down lower, she watched in horror as he tossed Kelsey to the ground. Her mate bounced and rolled a few times before coming to a halt.

Mythia roared and angled herself to free fall toward them. Her wings rested along her body to allow her to cut through quicker.

Xomor landed not too far from Kelsey. The blue dragon paced and kept his gaze on her.

Mythia landed on the ground. If it wasn't for Kelsey being positioned between them, she would have charged at him. She bared her fangs and growled. Her talons scraped the ground, itching to tear him limb from limb.

Getting to her feet, Kelsey stumbled before righting herself.

Mythia shot her gaze back to the blue dragon, now in his human form. He was dressed in fighting leathers, and had his large sword sheathed in the scabbard on his back.

She pulled back on her animal and transitioned to her human form. She too was dressed for battle, with her large daggers at her waist.

"You will die for touching her," Mythia snarled as she stalked toward Kelsey, eyeing her to see if there were any noticeable wounds. "Are you injured?"

Arriving at her side, Mythia ran her hands along her shoulders and arms, but didn't see anything life-threatening.

"I'm okay. Just a few scrapes from the fall." There were a few strands of grass in her hair and a scrape on her chin. Kelsey spun around and faced Xomor. "That's how you put me down? Just toss me like I'm some crap toy or something?"

Ignoring Kelsey, he strolled toward them

with a menacing expression on his face, his attention locked on Mythia.

"This is she? The one who touched the medallion and activated the spell?"

"She's none of your concern," Mythia growled, placing Kelsey behind her. The protective nature of her animal was growing strong. She had half a mind to exact vengeance upon him for every scratch on Kelsey's skin. She didn't care if he was her mate's ancestor.

"I would beg to differ," he grunted, stopping a few feet from Mythia. "Let me see her."

"No."

"I can speak for myself," Kelsey objected. She stood next to Mythia and folded her arms in front of her chest. She eyed Xomor warily, the distrust apparent on her face.

She shouldn't trust him.

"Do you know who I am, girl?"

"An idiot," Kelsey declared. Mythia had to admit, she was quite proud of her mate for not showing fear and standing up to Xomor. She would definitely have to reward her for her bravery.

"Watch your mouth, girl," he snarled.

"Watch yours." Mythia rested her hand on the hilt of her sword, issuing a warning growl.

"What did you want me to say? You're my great... I don't know how many greats grandfather? My ancestor?" Kelsey spat. She moved to stand in front of him and placed her hands on her waist. "Mythia told me of the curse. That whosoever held the medallion, you are bound to protect."

Mythia tensed at Kelsey's closeness to the other dragon. She kept her hand on the hilt of her weapon, prepared to defend her mate if necessary.

"Then you know why I am taking you away from Mythia. You are my responsibility."

"The hell I am. Where have you been all these years? Our family has suffered. Each generation has struggled to make ends meet." She poked him in his chest. His eyes widened as she continued on. "You know you have family, but you'll only come around to protect someone because of a necklace? Did you seek out our family to see if we needed help anyway? You were there when Paxton lost the necklace to Mythia."

"That is why I fought Mythia, to reclaim the —"

"It shouldn't have mattered about the necklace!" Kelsey hollered, her voice echoing through the air.

Xomor took a step back from her, but Kelsey pursued him. He flicked his gaze to Mythia in shock. Mythia bit back her laughter and slid her dagger back into its sheath. It may be Xomor who needed rescuing.

"But I am here now to take you away and—"

"I'm not leaving my mate." Kelsey pulled the neckline of her dress to the side to brandish her claiming mark. Mythia's chest puffed out with pride. Her mate was proud to have been claimed by her.

Xomor froze. He moved closer to Kelsey and took in her mark, then sniffed it.

His eyes met Mythia's.

"You are true mates." It wasn't a question, but a statement. He would be able to sense the bond between two people who were destined for each other. He stood up to his full height. "Then I have no claim."

"No, you don't." Mythia moved behind

Kelsey and wrapped an arm around her waist. "Now leave."

He stared at Kelsey for another moment before jerking his head in a nod. He spun on his heel and began walking away from them.

Mythia let out a deep breath. It was over, and she didn't have to kill in front of her mate. She pressed a kiss to Kelsey's head. She would take her mate home, and they would discuss her standing between two dragons.

"Wait!" Kelsey broke from Mythia's hold and raced after him.

CHAPTER FOURTEEN

Kelsey stopped suddenly when Xomor turned back to her with his gaze hard.

"That's it? You're just going to leave?" she panted, trying to catch her breath.

"What are you talking about, woman?"

"First of all, my name is Kelsey." Without looking, she could feel Mythia come to stand near her. It baffled her that he was just going to leave, and that was it.

"What are you asking, Kelsey?"

"I don't know. Don't you want to meet your other family? See how they are? Get to know them?" She looked up at the piercing blue sky. "Isn't it lonely living a long life and not getting to know any of your descendants?"

"You just said it. Dragons have long lives. We outlive many people. Without a mate, there is no other person to walk this earth with. We are better by ourselves." He jerked his chin toward the air behind her shoulder.

"But is it truly? Isn't it better to know them and love them than to never have any memories of them?" she asked softly, stepping forward. "I think it's honorable of you to honor a curse that someone put on you, but I think what makes a great dragon would be protecting those in his family because he wants to, and not because he's made to."

He stared at her for a moment before blinking.

"I haven't been the best person or easiest to get along with," he said.

Kelsey didn't miss Mythia's snort.

"But that's okay. I know my mom and grandmother would love to meet you. They would get a kick out of it. When Mythia confirmed that I have dragon's blood running through me, it made me realize that my mom even has dragon behavior. She collects things."

"What kind of things?" Mythia and Xomor echoed simultaneously.

"Things from our family that she's found. She's researched her family, but we've only been able to go back a few generations to Paxton Rose. I'm sure she would love to ask you questions."

"This is not my territory. I am not welcome here."

Kelsey spun around and moved over to Mythia. She stopped in front of her mate, who kept her eyes trained on Xomor.

"Mythia." She rested her hand on Mythia's chest, getting her attention. "Can he have permission to travel here for my family? For me?"

Something deep inside of her needed to find out the information he had about her family. Her heart wouldn't allow him to just walk away and never have a connection with his family. Now that she was the mate of a dragon, she would live as long as them. He wouldn't have to be alone again.

"What?" Mythia frowned. "Another

dragon is not needed to protect the area. This is my job."

"Paxton asked you to protect the area. I'm asking you to allow my kin to visit. Help my family."

"If your family needs help, then I shall—"

Kelsey placed a finger on her lips to shush her. Mythia was one stubborn dragon.

"I love how possessive you are, but this is something I need. My mom and grandmother will need. He's my family. Please, do this for me?" Mythia stared at her for what seemed like ages. If Kelsey was a full-blooded dragon who came from a long line of dragons, would they not be allowed to visit her?

"What do you think?" Mythia asked him.

"Without a mate, life has been lonely. Kelsey has stirred a curiosity in me. I would be honored to meet her family and help them in any way, because she's right. I should have looked out for my lineage without being made to."

Kelsey looked at the proud man before her. He didn't seem as scary as he had during her time walk.

"Then so be it. Xomor, you may come

and go to visit your kin. But do not bring trouble to these lands or—"

"You do not need to say it, Mythia. I would never want to bring harm to those who share my blood." He bowed deeply to Mythia, who strode forward and offered her hand to him.

Kelsey's heart skipped a beat as she watched them shake on the deal they'd just struck. Her mother and grandmother were going to love knowing that some of the old family tales were true.

"I must be going on my way."

"How will I get a hold of you?" Kelsey asked, doubting the dragon carried a cell phone around as he flew all over the world.

Reaching into a small pocket of his leathers, he stepped toward her. She held out her hand and gasped when he dropped a red gemstone into her hand.

"Hold that in your hand and call my name."

"Why rubies?" she asked. The blood-red stone was oval-shaped, smooth, and translucent, giving way to the hexagonal prisms underneath the surface. It was beautiful.

"It is my favorite stone. It reminds me of

the hair of the first woman I loved." He stared down at the stone, and Kelsey found herself intrigued by his story. It was one she believed he needed to share with them.

With a nod, he took one last look at her and spun around on his heel. He sprinted away toward the cliff and dove over the edge.

Kelsey screamed and took off after him. What the hell? Did he just—

She drew to an abrupt halt at the sight of his massive blue dragon flying off into the sky. Her heart was racing a mile a minute. She'd thought he had plummeted to his death.

"Are you all right?" Mythia asked, coming to stand next to Kelsey. "Why did you scream?"

"Did you not see him jump off the cliff?" Kelsey asked incredulously, clutching the stone in her hand.

"I do it all the time." Mythia snorted, waving off the action as if it were nothing. "That's not a big deal."

"What if you don't shift?"

"Why wouldn't I shift?" Mythia stared at her, giving her a slow blink. "You, my love, will need to meet my dragon. Once you do, you will understand me more."

"I'd love to meet your dragon."

"Good, because you're going to get your first flying session tonight." Mythia dropped a kiss to her lips.

"Really?"

"Yes."

Mythia sprinted fast toward the cliff. Kelsey's heart lodged in her throat at watching the love of her life jump off.

The roar of a dragon filled the air. The ground rumbled from the power of Mythia landing behind her. Kelsey whipped around and took in the beauty of the only dragon staring at her. She was amazed by the size of the beautiful beast.

She'd only ever seen Mythia's animal while she glided through the sky.

Her large head came to hover in front of Kelsey.

"My, you are a beauty," Kelsey murmured as she reached out her hand to touch Mythia's nose. The warmth she felt sent a rush of excitement through Kelsey. She took in the horn on Mythia's forehead, her ferocious fangs, and her large amber eyes. They glowed brightly as they took her in.

Kelsey didn't feel intimated or afraid of the dragon.

This was Mythia, her mate, and the dragon was part of her.

Snorting, she turned her body to where her wings were closest to Kelsey. She knelt down and leaned over, signaling for Kelsey to crawl on.

Kelsey never would've thought she'd actually get to ride a dragon. She used Mythia's shoulder to step up and crawl onto her back, then settled along the base of Mythia's neck. There were horn-like protrusions that gave her something to hold on to. They were far enough apart from each other that Kelsey could settle in between them, as if she were sitting on a saddle.

Mythia glanced back and looked at her.

Kelsey read her message loud and clear.

Hold on.

Grabbing the small horn in front of her, she blew out a shaky breath.

Mythia ran toward the edge and jumped off. Kelsey's scream was snatched away by the winds as she tightened her hold on the horn while Mythia swooped higher into the air.

Her wings were spread wide, allowing her to glide easily. The wind whipped through Kelsey's hair, the night air refreshing.

She looked around and took in the magnificent view. Montana was absolutely breathtaking from up here. There were barely any clouds in the sky. The moon was high, shining its bright rays.

There was no fear in her heart at these crazy heights.

This was something she would never forget.

Lucky enough for her, she would get to do this many times in her lifetime.

* * *

"That was amazing." Kelsey wrapped her arms around Mythia once she'd shifted back to her human form. They were on the landing deck of the castle. She was extremely pleased that her mate enjoyed their flight. She flew them around for a little while, sensing that her mate wasn't quite ready to descend.

The oversized animal was excited their mate wasn't afraid of her, and wanted to spend time with her.

"I'm glad you enjoyed yourself." Mythia paused, sensing a strong presence in the castle.

"What is it?" Kelsey asked.

"Someone is here." Security wasn't activated, and the grounds appeared to be quiet. She took Kelsey's hand and pulled her in close. She knew exactly where the uninvited guest was located.

"No tour this time?" Kelsey stepped closer and wrapped her arm around Mythia's waist.

"Not yet." She teleported them outside of her office. She didn't sense any devious intentions. What she did pick up on was the familiarity of the person on the other side of the door.

"That's something that'll take some time getting used to."

"Come." Mythia took her hand and opened the door. Once inside, Mythia drew to a halt as her eyes landed on her guest. A tall figure stood in front of the roaring fire burning in the hearth. "Galdar?"

"Hello, little sister." Galdar turned around with a grin on his face. It had been many years since they had seen each other. He had grown a beard. His dark hair was in locks that were pulled back away from his face. His golden-brown skin was smooth and flawless. He was dressed in the attire of the people from the region he lived. Long robes that reached his ankles and showcased his sandaled feet. "I hear congratulations are in order."

Relaxing, Mythia tugged Kelsey to her side and quickly made introductions.

"What are you doing here?" she then demanded, motioning for Kelsey to have a seat on the couch near the fireplace. She went without objection and sat, her wide eyes darting between Galdar and Mythia.

She and her brother strolled over to the fireplace.

"You are forever direct. Can you not be happy to see your elder brother?" he joked.

"It's been fifty years since we've seen each other. I send one message to request your assistance with something. I don't hear back from you, and then you randomly appear. Excuse me for being a little concerned."

"That is true. I did as you requested and looked into the history of your mate," he advised her. Mythia ignored Kelsey's shocked gasp.

"And? What did you find out?" Mythia was tense. Kelsey, being the ancestor of Xomor, was not worthy of her brother coming this far.

"I'm sure you have learned about her connection with Xomor. I'm sure it was exciting to meet your ancestor that helped start your family line. Did you know his first love was a human? He had three children with her, but they were not fated mates. Such a story to hear."

Kelsey was sitting on the edge of her seat, her attention focused solely on Galdar. Her brother was a history buff and very knowledgeable, but he also loved attention, as well as hear himself speak.

"The point of why you're here," Mythia attempted to redirect him.

"Ah, yes. Why I traveled thousands of miles." Reaching into his robe, he pulled out a manilla envelope and handed it to Kelsey.

"Ms. Rose, you never knew who your father was."

"No. He left before my mother knew she was pregnant with me. She was never able to find him to tell him." Kelsey stared at the envelope with wide eyes. "Is he alive?"

"I'm afraid not, my dear. He passed about six months after he left Saxon Hills. But that is not why I came all this way. Your father was half human, half dragon. His father was a dragon shifter. You have more dragon in your blood than you thought."

Kelsey's gaze flew to Mythia's.

More of the pieces fell into place.

Mythia turned to Galdar. "Thank you, brother."

"It's my pleasure to be here and meet my sister-in-law, and to also bring her information on her relatives. You will find everything in there about him and his family. I'm sure they will be open to meeting you, as you are his only child."

Kelsey wiped away the tears that trailed down her cheeks.

"I have traveled many miles and need to rest. Antha told me she was preparing a room for me, so I will bid you both a good night." With a nod, he left the room.

"Are you all right?" Mythia knelt before Kelsey. She didn't like to see the wet trails on her face.

"Yes, I'm fine. It's just so much in a short span of time." She barked out a laugh and placed the envelope and ruby on the couch next to her.

Mythia cupped her cheek and rested her forehead against Kelsey's. "I'm here for you."

"I know, and I love you for it."

Pulling back, she stared into Kelsey's eyes. She couldn't believe what she was hearing. Proclaiming to love someone was a human tradition, and her heart warmed.

"You do?" she asked.

"Yes." Reaching for Mythia, she tugged her close. "To think I came here to steal something back from you. But in the end, it was you who stole from me."

"What did I steal?" Mythia asked, brushing Kelsey's hair away from her face so she could gaze upon her beauty.

"My heart."

EPILOGUE

"Hold your hand out to him. He'll come to you." Kelsey giggled. She and Mythia had arrived to help out on the farm. Once the initial shock of mating with a dragon had settled, Kelsey had brought Mythia to the farm to meet her mother and grandmother. Delaney and Chana both loved Mythia.

Jasper even came around to Mythia once he got to know her.

"The beast will not come to me. He's afraid of me."

"Well, if you weren't staring at him like you wanted to burn him, he would." Kelsey took the apple from Mythia and walked a few steps ahead. The horse, Charlie, trotted forward and nibbled on the apple in her hand. "You've got to be gentle with him. They can sense your true nature."

"Of course he can." Mythia folded her arms over her chest. "He knows a predator when he sees one."

It was a beautiful day to be outside. They had finished their chores, and everyone was relaxing.

Not too long after their altercation with Xomor did she finally call on him. The meeting between him and her family was interesting. He was able to shed a lot of light on the artifacts her mother had collected. He had even brought her a few as gifts the first day they'd met.

Xomor had honored the agreement with Mythia and had brought no trouble to their town. He had become a member of their family, and even showed up often to help out on the farm.

Kelsey glanced over to the house and found Delaney, Chana, and Xomor sitting on the back porch, conversing. Warmth filled her heart that she had not only returned the ruby medallion to her mother, but had given her so much more.

Xomor would now forever have a family he could be a part of. Since joining theirs, he'd started searching for other members of his lineage. This was right up Delaney and Chana's alley. They loved researching family trees. They had hit a roadblock before, but now, with Xomor's help, they had infinite resources and leads.

Charlie finished his apple and moved on to graze. Kelsey tossed the core and walked over to Mythia.

"Thank you."

Mythia frowned. "What have I done?"

"Just for being you. I'm so happy."

Everything in her life was perfect. She couldn't think of a better outcome from the first night she'd met Mythia. She wrapped her arm around her as they strolled along in a comfortable silence. The Rose Farm was a beautiful piece of land, and in the fall, the colors were bold and picturesque.

They arrived at a wide tree that overlooked the corral where the cattle were. Mythia leaned back against it and pulled Kelsey flush to her.

"I've been wanting to get you alone for a while," Mythia confessed, pressing a chaste kiss to Kelsey's lips.

"I'm sure you have."

The mating call was still just as strong. It took great restraint to keep her hands off her mate, because her body always responded to Mythia.

At the moment, she was already on fire. Mythia's hand slid around to her ass and cupped it. Even through her jeans, she could feel the heat from Mythia's touch.

"Do you think they'll miss us?" Mythia murmured, pressing another kiss to her lips. She trailed hot, open-mouthed kisses along Kelsey's jawline and down to her neck. The sensation of her tongue licking over her claiming mark sent a jolt of lightning to her core.

"What do you have in mind?" Kelsey moaned, arching into Mythia as she clasped her fingers together at the base of Mythia's neck. She already knew what her mate wanted, and she wanted it too.

She tried to think of where they could sneak away to for some alone time. Six months had passed since they'd mated, and the intense need to be consumed by her mate was still as strong. The barn was always an easy place to sneak girls into when she was a teenager. She could have Mythia teleport them there, where no one would bother looking for them.

"Close your eyes," Mythia ordered. She lifted her head and leveled Kelsey with her intense amber eyes that were blazing with desire. Her deep, husky voice was commanding. Kelsey instantly did as she was instructed.

Air blew past her and she shivered.

"Open them," Mythia said.

No longer feeling Mythia near her, Kelsey opened her eyes and gasped. They were no longer on the farm, but in a secluded area, the sound of water filling her ears. She looked in the direction of it and stood in awe at the sight before her. They were somewhere private, with lush greenery surrounded them. The water was blue and clear. She could practically see the bottom of the natural pool, even as steam rose from the water's edge.

She took in her naked mate standing at

the edge of the spring. Kelsey glanced down and found she was naked too.

"This place is beautiful." She spun around and took in the beauty of nature. She was in awe of the power of her mate. Mythia had consistently ensured she was well taken care of. Each day that passed, she had fallen more in love with Mythia.

Mythia held out her hand. "Come to me, Kelsey."

Her feet began carrying her toward her mate. There was nowhere she wouldn't go with this woman.

Thank you for reading!

* * * * *

If you enjoyed this story, then you will love the Nightstar Shifters series. Find this collection by visiting Ariel's website. www.thearielmarie.com

A Letter From The Author

Dear Reader,

Thank you for taking the time to read my book! I hope you enjoyed reading The Dragon and Her Thief. It was a short story recently featured in an anthology. I decided to release it on its own so that those who didn't purchase the Cocky Alpha Shifters anthology may enjoy it.

Happy reading,
Ariel Marie

The Nightstar Shifters

No wolf can resist the call to mate.

Strong female wolves are in search of their mate. The desire is strong for these women who long to find the one person meant for them.

They are fierce and determined, putting their trust in fate.

If you love lesbian wolf shifter romance filled with action and adventure, then you will love the Nightstar Shifters series

* * *

Find this collection by visiting Ariel's website.
www.thearielmarie.com

About the Author

Ariel Marie is an author who loves the paranormal, action and hot steamy romance. She combines all three in each and every one of her stories. For as long as she can remember, she has loved vampires, shifters and every creature you can think of. This even rolls over into her favorite movies. She loves a good action packed thriller! Throw a touch of the supernatural world in it and she's hooked!

She grew up in Cleveland, Ohio where she currently resides with her husband and three beautiful children.

For more information:
www.thearielmarie.com

Also by Ariel Marie

<u>The Nightstar Shifters</u>

Sailing With Her Wolf

Protecting Her Wolf

Sealed With A Bite

Hers to Claim

Wanted by the Wolf

Taming Her Mate

<u>The Immortal Reign series</u>

Deadly Kiss

Iced Heart

Royal Bite

<u>Blackclaw Alphas (Reverse Harem Series)</u>

Fate of Four

Bearing Her Fate (TBD)

<u>The Midnight Coven Brand</u>

Forever Desired

Wicked Shadows

Saving Penny

A Beary Christmas

Howl for Me

Birthright

Return to Darkness

Red and the Alpha